SHIP OF DREAMS

BEN ARMSTRONG

{armstrob}

This book is a work of fiction. Any references to historical events, real people, or real places are used fictitiously. Other names, characters, places, and events are products of the author's imagination, and any resemblance to actual events or places or persons, living or dead, is entirely coincidental.

First edition

ISBN: 978-1-7342597-8-0

For my Family

"I cannot imagine any condition which would cause a ship to founder. I cannot conceive of any vital disaster happening to this vessel. Modern shipbuilding has gone beyond that."

- CAPTAIN EDWARD SMITH, 1907

CONTENTS

INTRODUCTION

My fascination with the Titanic began when I was nine or ten years old. It started with a game called *Titanic: Adventure Out of Time*. Released in 1996, it was a point and click game that had you playing as a British spy who was sent back in time to complete a mission in order to prevent WWI. The game involved exploring the ship, solving puzzles, and listening closely to what people told you as this could greatly impact the outcome of the game.

Back then, I don't know that I ever actually beat the game. It was hard for me to remember what a certain person had said, so I would get stuck at one spot or another, and then I'd lose. I didn't mind, though. I fondly remember playing the game for countless hours, and likely bugging my mother with endless questions (sorry, Mom). But, this truly was where my fascination with the ship began.

And then of course, James Cameron released his 1997 movie, *Titanic*, which renewed most of the world's interest in the ship and her story. I remember watching it as a kid, but I was more interested in seeing the ship in such great detail than

I was the story. For the time, it was an incredible achievement by Cameron.

Throughout my teenage years and into adulthood, my interest in the ship waned on and off, but it was always there to some extent. Not long ago, I rediscovered the game that started it all and got it running on a modern PC—what a treat that was. I was over the moon with excitement to be able to play the game again. As it turns out, the game is much easier when you're in your thirties as opposed to nine or ten. Nevertheless, I cherished my time back on board Titanic, talking to people (remembering what they told me), and actually solving the puzzles and successfully completing my mission.

The main character in the story you're about to read isn't meant to be me, however, I think you'll find without too much effort that we both share a passion for Titanic. This story was a lot of fun for me to write, and while I know it won't be for everyone, I hope you get at least a little something from it. And for those of you who also love Titanic, I think you'll have a great time. Either way, thank you as always for your continued support of my writing. It means more to me than I could ever say in words on a page.

Welcome aboard!

PROLOGUE

HARLAND & WOLFF, 1907

William James Pirrie, owner of Harland & Wolff, met with James Bruce Ismay, the chairman of The White Star Line, during the summer of 1907. This meeting was to discuss the plan to build a class of immense luxury passenger ships. They were to be the biggest ships the world had ever seen.

The reason for such a plan was due to their rival, The Cunard Line, having debuted their two new ships; the Lusitania and Mauretania. The former being the largest ship at the time until the latter was built three months later. Both ships were nearly 800 feet long and propelled the Cunard Line ahead of White Star. This, for obvious reasons, would not stand with Mr. Ismay.

It was devised at the meeting in 1907 that three ships were to be built by Harland and Wolff; The Olympic, The Titanic, and later, The Britannic. These massive ships, which would be over 100 feet longer than either of Cunard's newest, would focus on luxury and comfort instead of sheer speed. That being said, Titanic would be clocked at over twenty-three knots during one of her sea trials, which at the time was a very reputable pace, especially given her great size.

Construction on the first ship, Olympic, was started on 16 December 1908, and on her sister ship, Titanic, three months later. Britannic's keel wouldn't be laid until 30 November 1911, with her completion date being 12 December 1915. This delay was two-fold, the primary reason being a lack of space at the shipyard for three of these colossal ships to be built simultaneously. The other reason being, as many may already know, was the sinking of the Titanic. After the tragedy and following inquiries, numerous changes were proposed and implemented in both Olympic and Britannic.

While many people, particularly those with a love of history, know of Olympic and Britannic, you would be hard pressed to find someone who doesn't know of Titanic and her short and tragic maiden voyage. Even today, over 110 years after the sinking, her story still continues to fascinate people around the world.

CHAPTER I

1

It was August of 2019—the beginning of another school year at Redfield High School. As usual, the seniors in my morning History class were ever so slowly taking their seats, struggling just to maintain consciousness. While I felt history was important, I agreed with my students that classes shouldn't start any earlier than nine a.m. Nevertheless, that particular decision was above my pay grade, and so I always tried to make the best of the early morning lessons.

"Good morning, class," I said, a moment after the final tardy bell rang. I stood in front of my desk and looked at the twenty-one seniors in attendance. As expected, they were all still trying to wake up—most had a coffee or energy drink glued to their hand. The school prohibited drinks (water being the exception) in the classroom, but the way I saw it, my classroom, my rules. I wouldn't want to try and learn at eight in the morning without some assistance from Mr. Caffeine, so why should they?

"Good morning, Mr. Lawson."

I raised my own coffee to the class in a cheer. "I hope everyone had a good summer break. And just to reassure all of you, for the first few days I like to keep things light, give everyone a chance to readjust to the whole learning thing."

I smiled at them, seeing relief on many of their faces. I knew history was far from anyone's favorite subject. There were exceptions, of course, but in general it ranked right up there with calculus and accounting.

I started teaching history at RHS back in 2009 at the tender age of twenty-one. Looking back, I still can't believe they let me teach students who were a mere three years younger than myself. However, fast forward ten years and I have been awarded teacher of the year for eight years in a row, so I must be doing okay. If I had to guess, my popularity as a teacher (at least with the students) is due to my willingness to not only listen to their wants and needs, but the fact that I actively encourage them to ask questions and to advocate for what particular events in history they want to learn about. With one exception, and I'll get to that in due time, I create my teaching curriculum around what my class wants to study. It's unique, and I know at least a few of my colleagues vehemently disagree with it, but I stand by my methods and their results—I also go back to my earlier point of my classroom, my rules.

2

As promised to my class, the first two days were kept light in terms of actual learning. I chatted with them about their summer adventures, as well as just getting to know them in general. A few of them seemed eager to start learning (there usually were a few), and others seemed just fine with enjoying the coffee and casual conversation the entire school year. I was laid back, but even I couldn't justify the latter, so on day three it was time to figure out what was on the agenda for the year.

"So, what do you guys want to learn about this year?" What I expected, and what indeed happened, was a room full of silent and confused students staring back at me. I laughed. "I guess nobody told you about my History class huh? No worries, I'll explain.

"My teaching style is based on the idea that you shouldn't have to learn things you don't want to. I have one exception to this, and we'll get to that later, but aside from that I want to know what parts of history you'd like to learn about."

After another moment of continued silence, one girl raised her hand. I nodded to her.

"Can we learn about 9/11?"

A few murmurs sprouted up among the class, and it sounded like they were in agreement with wanting to learn about this topic. I wasn't surprised at this request. Despite history ranking low on the overall list of subjects, there were always a few particular moments and events that I get asked to cover—9/11 being near the top. It's followed closely by the JFK Assassination, as well as the MLK Assassination. All of which I am happy to include in my curriculum.

"Of course," I said, jotting it down on my notepad. The girl who had asked was named Jenny, Jenny Willard if I recall correctly. I had had her sister in my class a few years back, and she was the spitting image of her. "Anyone else?" There was more silence, and after a few minutes I decided to break it. "Okay, no problem. We'll cover 9/11 later on this year, but the first lesson will be the exception I mentioned earlier. How many of you are familiar with the story of The Titanic?"

Most of their hands went up, which wasn't too surprising. The tragic story of that ship was widely known around the world. While the death count was nowhere near that of either World Wars, the 1918 flu pandemic that followed a few years later, or even of 9/11, Titanic still remains to this day one of the most well-known tragedies in history. And the truth is, most people don't know the half of it.

I saw we still had about twenty minutes left of class, so I thought I'd open it up for discussion on the topic. "So, tell me, do any of you know some facts about Titanic?" To my surprise, several hands went up. "Oh wow, that's great. Uh, how about you, Kent?"

"It hit an iceberg on its maiden voyage at sea and sank." *As good of a place to start as any,* I thought to myself.

"That's correct," I said. "Who else?" Jenny from earlier raised her hand and I pointed to her.

"Weren't there like, a lot of rich people on it?" *Interesting. Not a fact I thought would come up.*

I nodded. "That's right, quite a few actually. Where'd you hear that?"

She shrugged. "My parents watched the movie quite a bit, and when I happened to be in the room I saw a bunch of people in fancy clothing."

Ah yes, the famous 1997 movie, *Titanic*, brought to us by James Cameron. I've heard there are some history buffs who absolutely hate his take on the event, but I myself quite enjoy it. The sheer amount of detail and passion he put into the film are a testament to his skills as a producer. While it's true the love story between Jack and Rose never really happened, there were several parts of the movie based on actual events.

"I'm glad you mentioned the movie, Jenny. I always make it a point to show it to students during the first semester. The truth is, the richest man alive at that time was onboard the Titanic. His name was John Jacob Astor, and in today's money he would have a net worth of nearly two billion dollars."

I realized then that I was on the verge of starting to ramble. Looking at the clock I saw class was nearly finished, so I walked back around my desk and sat down. "Well, I'll leave it at that for today. I have a soft spot for Titanic, and I've been known to be a bit long-winded on the topic. Feel free to use your phones for the last ten minutes of class while I work on our curriculum for the year."

3

The rest of my morning classes were uneventful. At lunch, I walked into the teacher's lounge and spotted Josh sitting at one of the tables near the corner. As I joined him, he greeted me with a wave and continued eating his meal—I think it was spaghetti that day.

"Morning, Andrew."

"Morning," I said, taking out the simple ham and cheese sandwich I had brought. "How are things in the digital world today?"

Josh Flintwood was our system administrator. He was forty years old and a wizard behind a keyboard. He could be a bit eccentric at times, particularly when you got him onto the topic of computers, but he was one of the good ones. We've been friends for eight years, almost my entire career at RHS.

Josh sighed. "The beginning of the school year is always the worst. Teachers needing help with getting into their computers, students trying to access restricted sites on their tablets, and of course our fearless leader trying to give me advice on how we should increase our security."

"But you love that stuff," I said, taking a bite of my sandwich.

He smiled and nodded. "I do, but that doesn't mean I can't complain about it."

"Fair."

"How goes the trek through history so far?" he asked, slurping up a generous helping of his spaghetti. I knew all too well that this question was merely a formality, asked out of courtesy to me. Josh couldn't care less about anything involving history. Nevertheless, I always took advantage of an opportunity to talk about it.

"So far so good. It's only day three, so I'm just starting to map out a plan for the year. We'll cover Titanic, of course, and it sounds like they want to learn about 9/11 as well. I'll probably throw in a lecture or two on JFK towards the end of the year. That usually keeps their attention before Summer break."

"You and that ship. I'll never understand your fascination with it."

This was a conversation we'd had countless times, and it always went the same way. He'd wonder why I enjoyed the topic so much, I'd try to explain how tragic the sinking had been and what it would have been like to experience it first-hand, and then he'd shrug it off. I'll save you the replay of this particular rendition of the conversation—it was indeed the same as I described.

We spent the rest of our lunch discussing miscellaneous topics, none of which would be of any interest to you, so I'll again save you from the details and get on with the story. The first bell rang, signaling there were fifteen minutes left of lunch. This was my queue to head back to my classroom and prepare for that afternoon's classes.

"Better get back to it," I said, standing up and pushing my chair in "Hey, do you want to grab a drink after work?"

Josh nodded. "That sounds great. Four thirty? Usual place?"

"You got it. Have a good afternoon."

4

My first class after lunch was sophomore American History. While I'd love nothing more than to share my fascination with Titanic to any and all who would listen, I managed enough restraint to only do so to my senior students. I was in the middle of giving an overview of the Civil War when a knock came at my door—it was superintendent Jackson, and behind him was an older gentleman, who looked to be in his late 70s.

The man was wearing a pair of grey slacks and a black sweater. His hair was what first caught my attention, though. It was salt and pepper colored, more salt than pepper, and I got the feeling he hadn't bothered with styling it in a long time —which was somehow fitting.

"Ah, superintendent Jackson, how can I help?"

He cleared his throat. "Andrew, could we have a word?" I felt the first wave of panic course through me at that moment. The superintendent's first name was Bob. He's a nice enough guy, sometimes a little too 'by the book' for my taste, but overall not bad. One thing I knew for sure was that he'd never use my first name in front of students—not unless it was urgent.

"Of course," I said, turning to my class. "Go ahead and read a few pages in your textbooks while I'm gone."

I stepped out into the hallway with Bob and the older

man, wondering what on earth this could be about. The man motioned toward an empty class room across the hall. As the door was shut behind me, I was instructed to have a seat, and the two left me in the room—this added to my confusion. A few minutes later, the door opened and the man from earlier stepped inside. He must have told Bob his presence was no longer needed.

"Hi, Andrew," said the man as he sat down in a chair across from us. "I apologize for the secrecy, but what we're here to discuss is highly classified. Do you understand?"

I nodded, although I'd be lying if I said I wasn't nervous about what I just walked into.

"Good." He took out a small device, no bigger than a pack of playing cards, and sat it down in the middle of the table. He pressed a button on the side of it and a low frequency hum emanated from the device for a few seconds before turning silent once again. "This is a frequency disruptor. It will ensure our conversation is not overheard by anyone outside of this room."

I frowned. "If I may ask, what could possibly concern me that is so secretive? I'm just a history teacher at a small high school. The most exciting thing that happens here is when we get a new type of food in the cafeteria."

The man nodded his understanding. "Yes, that's right, you're just a history teacher at a small school. It'll all make sense soon, I promise." He reached into his pocket and pulled out another device. This one looked like an iPhone but bulkier. "Are you familiar at all with the concept of time travel?"

Looking back at that afternoon in the empty classroom with this mysterious man, I wondered how different my life would have been had I simply chosen not to listen to what he had to say. It would have been easy enough—just stand up and walk out. I wasn't under arrest or anything like that. There was nothing keeping me in that chair, but for whatever reason I chose to stay. The memory of that afternoon lives rent free in my mind these days, for reasons you yourself will find out soon enough.

The man in the black sweater stared at me from across the table, waiting for some sort of response. After a moment, I managed to say something.

"Uh, well, I've seen the Back to the Future movies. Does that count for something?" I forced a laugh, but I saw the man was just staring blankly at me, so I tried a different approach. "I know it isn't possible. The sheer amount of power you'd need isn't something we can technologically achieve… at least not yet."

The man shook his head and pointed at the device. "That, my friend, is called an Anode Reactor, a time machine if you will. I helped invent the prototype about a decade ago, and have perfected it in the last couple years."

Had I heard him right? Surely not. He's invented a device capable of time travel? My mind started to race with the possibilities of such a feat. *We could go anywhere*, I thought. I realized I was zoning out and forced myself back to the present conversation.

"How?" I asked. "How is that possible?"

He smiled and picked up the device. "I think it's best if I just show you. Are you up for a demonstration?"

Now that I have time to reflect on this particular moment, I realize how few questions I asked this man. Sure, in the coming pages you'll see I do ask many more, but prior to allowing myself to be a part of such a risky demonstration, I asked frighteningly few questions.

That being said, I think the reason was—a tiny part of me thought, *what if he's not crazy?* I couldn't fathom the idea of actually being able to travel back in time—the implications of such an ability were beyond my comprehension. In other words—you bet your life I wanted to see a demonstration.

"Let's see it."

"Where would you like to go? Or, more aptly, when would you like to go?"

What a question, I thought. Giving a history teacher the opportunity to visit any time period—any at all. It was an overwhelming decision, one I wasn't ready to make.

I shrugged. "I wouldn't know where to start. Whatever you pick would be fine."

The man thought for a moment as he tapped out a few commands on the device, and I began to hear a high pitched noise, but it quickly faded away. After another few seconds, he stood up and walked to the center of the room, motioning for me to join him.

"The Anode Reactor will pull in anything within the set radius, so I'd prefer not to take the desk and chairs with us. Please stand next to me and remain as still as possible."

I was still quite skeptical about the whole situation, but being the history buff I was, even the most infinitesimal of chances that this man could let me see the past made it worthwhile to humor him.

"Say, you never told me your name," I said, standing next to the man, my heart beating out of my chest.

The man smiled. "James. James Kern."

He activated the device and the classroom at RHS disappeared in a blinding flash of light. I felt as if I had left my physical body and was now floating around as a wisp or something, and then everything came rushing back at me in a *wooshing* sound. A moment later, we were standing in what appeared to be a dusty warehouse of some sort.

"Welcome to the past," said James. "You can walk around a little if you'd like, but be careful not to touch anything. Butterfly effect and all that. Oh, and take it slow. The first few jumps are a little harsh on the body. You might feel a little nauseous." He smiled again.

Nauseous was right. I immediately keeled over and vomited my lunch. My stomach felt like it was doing somersaults, but I finally managed to compose myself and started to take in my surroundings. I walked to the edge of the room we were in and peered out one of the windows, of which there were many. I didn't need to do this to know where we were, but I wanted to at least get a glimpse of the sky, and of the famous grassy knoll. *Holy shit, this guy might still be crazy, but he really did figure out time travel.*

"Christ," I said. "We're in Dallas, 1963. This building is the School Book Depository. We're at the moment in time when JFK was assassinated."

James smiled and nodded. "I knew you'd pick up on it. It's actually November 20th, two days prior to the assassination. For obvious reasons I didn't bring us to the actual date. But, the fact you realized where we were so quickly is why I came to your school in the first place. Come on, let's get back to our time."

I stepped towards him, and a moment later another blinding light brought us back to RHS, 2019. We were back in the same classroom we had left, still intact from what I could tell. I still couldn't quite believe it—I lived to see the day we could travel back in time. If nothing else happened that day, I could die a happy man—and I meant that.

6

As the two of us sat down again at the table, I couldn't help but remember what James had said just before we returned from 1963. '*That's why I came to your school in the first place*' he had said. What did he mean by that? Looking back now, it made sense of course, but at the time I hadn't the slightest idea of what it meant.

"I read your book," said James, turning off his Anode Reactor and putting it back inside his pocket. "*Titanic: A Tragedy at Sea.* It was quite an enjoyable read I must say."

He read my book—I'll be honest, that was the last thing I had been thinking of in terms of reasons for him to be here. A moment later, as if my brain just needed a moment to catch up, I suddenly knew why he was here—knew why he'd shown me the Anode Reactor.

"I know why you're here," I said.

He nodded. "You're a smart man, Andrew. I figured it wouldn't take long."

"You want me to stop the Titanic from sinking."

He nodded again.

As the words escaped my mouth—words that encompassed a question I'd been asking myself for years, I felt my heart begin to race. Could something like this really be done? Stopping one of the most well-known maritime disasters from ever happening—it felt like a pipe dream.

"I—I don't know," I said. "Is something like that even possible?"

"Were we not just in 1963 a few moments ago?" asked

James. "And then in mere seconds back in this classroom? That was no dream. It really happened, I can assure you. I can take you somewhere else if you'd like further proof. I have nothing but time."

I couldn't help but grin at the pun, but my brain just couldn't wrap itself around the concept.

"It's not that," I said. "While I'll admit you've changed my mind on time travel being possible, which is awesome by the way, how can you actually change the past? I've read that if you change something it'll create some kind of parallel universe as opposed to ours. Is that not the case? I don't know, I'm quite a bit out of my element here."

James nodded. "It's a fair question, but that's a common misconception surrounding time travel. As you can imagine, it is a complicated process. I won't go too far into the details, at least not here, but what I can tell you is, most of the articles you'll find out there on time travel are wrong."

He stopped for a moment, and if I recall correctly, the look I saw on his face was of profound regret.

"I know they're wrong because, for better or worse, I've changed the past on more than one occasion. Trust me, it can be changed. And in the case of the Titanic, changing its fate will save more than the 1,500 who lost their lives the night of April 14th, 1912."

CHAPTER II

1

Titanic: A tragedy at Sea was a book I had written three years earlier. I didn't know whether or not those pages would ever see the light of day, but by the time I was done I had 120,000 words of Titanic history. It started off going over in detail the most widely agreed upon tale of how the ship met its fate. After that, I dove into some of the conspiracy theories (of which there are many) around how it sank, and whether or not (excuse the pun) they hold any water.

When I finished my final draft, I was surprised how quickly I found a publisher. The book didn't become a New York Times bestseller or anything, but it has done better than I could ever have imagined. Being written by a high school history teacher with a fascination bordering on an obsession with the ship, my expectations were quite low. Fast forward to 2019, and I was in an empty classroom with whom I'm quite certain is a crazy scientist, one who wants me to go back in time and change history. How could I say no?

2

My head was still spinning as I tried to understand just how the past could be changed. I remember repeating the last sentence James had said regarding more lives than the 1,500 lost in the sinking would be saved. What other lives did he mean? Did the sinking of the Titanic cause some kind of domino effect throughout history? If so, it wasn't anything I was familiar with.

"What happens to the rest of history if she doesn't sink?" I asked. "Does WW1 not happen or something? Surely a ship sinking wouldn't prevent something as big as that."

He shook his head. "No, unfortunately. As long as there are humans and weapons, there will be wars in which the former uses the latter to inflict pain on other humans."

I nodded in agreement, knowing all too well that we humans love our wars. The more I thought about it, I couldn't picture what a world without the Titanic sinking would be like. While it was a major event, would history really be changed in a dramatic way?

"So, why risk going back and stopping it? If we'll still have wars and everything they bring along with them, what's the point?" I knew that sounded insensitive. 1,500 people lost their lives, after all, but I was trying to think in terms of the bigger picture. Still, I did feel bad thinking about my phrasing of it.

James's expression suddenly darkened as he leaned forward, his eyes solemn and locked onto mine. "For you to truly understand, I need you to come with me to my lab." He disabled the frequency disruptor and stood up from the table, acting as if there was nothing more to discuss and that I was to follow him at once.

He has a lab? Of course he does. My brain was already hurting from my conversation with James, and I felt a trip to his lab wasn't going to help matters any. That being said, I couldn't help but feel a strong need to know just what exactly he had to show me. *A world where the Titanic doesn't sink,* I thought. While I desperately wanted to see what that world would look like, I needed time to think. Despite what my Titanic obsessed brain was telling me, I somehow managed to restrain myself from immediately going with this crazy man to his lab, which was who knows where.

"I—I don't know," I said, hesitating. "Can I think about it?"

He nodded. "Of course, take all the time you need." He pulled out a card from his back pocket and handed it to me. "Call me when you've made a decision, even if it's a no, I'd like to hear from you."

I took the card, feeling like I'd let him down. "I'll let you know soon. I just need some time to take this all in."

He put his hand on my shoulder and met my gaze. "Andrew, seriously, I get it. It's not like I'm asking you to drive me to the airport. Take time to think it over and give me a call, day or night. Okay?"

I nodded. "You'll hear from me soon."

A moment later, James left the room, leaving me with its empty silence. I somehow had to go back to class and finish out my day. My hopes weren't high, but thankfully I only had about an hour left. Still, I remember it being the longest hour I'd ever spent in a classroom.

3

After managing to make it through the rest of my day, I had to cancel my plans to have a drink with Josh. He understood, of course, but I still felt bad. I hated having to cancel plans, but I knew this wasn't something I could talk to him about, and I shuddered at the thought of spending another hour or two avoiding the topic. Instead, I picked up a pizza and some alcohol on my way home. Typical single guy thing to do, right?

I was ravenous by the time I made it home, so I quickly consumed the pizza while having my first round of gin and tonic. I grabbed the personal copy of my book, another gin and tonic, and sat down at the desk in my library. I remember finishing that entire second drink while staring at the book cover. I think at least part of me already knew I was going to say yes, I just hadn't been able to convince myself completely yet.

After pouring myself another drink, I wandered around my house, which was a modest three bedroom, two bath rambler, thinking about the conversion from earlier with James. The house, while not huge, was much too big for a single guy like myself. *What if something goes wrong?* I thought. *But, what if I succeed? History would be changed forever.*

I found my way back to the library and fell into one of the chairs. I picked up my book again, flipping through the pages, thinking back to all the time I spent typing out those words. *You know what you have to do. You were practically born for this.* A moment later I put the book back on its shelf, turned out the lights in the library, and made myself one more drink for the night.

I had made my decision.

4

The next morning, as I started teaching my Senior history class about the Titanic, my mind was continuously thinking about my conversation with James. It proved to be most difficult focusing on teaching the same historic event that I was just recently given the opportunity to change. Surreal doesn't quite cover the feeling I had that morning, however, I managed to get through it.

Just before lunch, I managed to catch my boss in his office. I told him I needed the rest of the day off, and mentioned it was in regard to the visitor I had the day before. As I expected, he understood. He didn't know what was going on with me or the strange man, but he trusted me, and that was enough for him.

"Good luck with whatever is going on, Andrew," he said. "Let me know if there's anything I can do to help."

I nodded. "Thank you, I will."

A moment later I headed outside the school to call James. I took out the card he gave me, dialed the number listed and waited.

"Hello, this is James," said a voice in my ear.

"Hey, it's Andrew."

I heard typing in the background, which quickly stopped. "Ah, Andrew, nice to hear from you. How are things?"

I ignored his question. "I've decided to do it."

"I knew you would." I felt I could hear the smirk on his face. *Of course he knew.*

"So, what now? Do you want me to meet you at your lab? Wherever that is."

"No need, Andrew. Give me five minutes and I'll come get you. Are you at the school?"

I didn't think too much about it at the time, but I'm now realizing that he said he'd come get me in five minutes, even though he didn't know for sure where I was. Hindsight and all that, I suppose.

"I am, yeah, just outside the main door."

A bit more typing. "Okay. If you don't mind, could you go wait in the same classroom we met in yesterday?"

"Uh, yeah… sure, I guess so. Five minutes you said?"

"Yup, that should be enough. See you shortly."

The call disconnected.

A moment later I was sitting back at the table in the same empty classroom I had first met James. Did I have any idea what awaited me? No. Looking back, I didn't have a clue what the future (or in this particular case, the past) held for me. Even if I had, however, part of me thinks I still would do it all over again, given the choice.

I was passing the time on my phone when the room suddenly filled with a blinding white light, followed by the appearance of James, who was now standing in front of the table. I dropped my phone on the table as I nearly fell out of the chair I had been sitting in. It took all my strength to bring the chair back down to four legs.

"Jesus, what the hell man?" I blurted out, feeling my heart pounding in my chest. "H—how did you… how are you here right now?" I didn't realize it right away, but after a moment I saw that I had gotten up and was standing against the wall.

He must have seen how startled I was, because he put up both his hands in *surrender* motion. "I'm sorry, Andrew, I see now I should have given you a heads up of my plan."

I wanted to speak, but my mouth wouldn't cooperate, so James continued.

"Are you okay? Do you need a minute, or should we get going to my lab?"

After what felt like ages, my heart started to calm itself. "How did you do that? You just suddenly appeared."

"Ah, yes," he said, pulling out the same device from yesterday. "While its primary purpose is time travel, the Anode Reactor is also capable of teleportation.

I stood in silence at first, unable to truly process what I had just heard. *Seriously?* I thought. *Time travel AND teleportation? What does this guy need me for? I think he's more than capable.* I didn't say this, mind you, at least not so directly, and not at that time.

"Are you really okay?" he asked, a look of legitimate concern appearing on his face. "I hope I didn't startle you too badly."

I finally managed words. "No, no, I'm fine. This is just... I mean, I'm still somewhat coming around to time travel, and now teleportation. I guess I shouldn't be surprised... if you can do one, why not the other. But still..." I trailed off, not really knowing where my thought process was going.

"Understandable, and I do apologize for springing it on you like this. I'll do my best to take things slower going forward. Think you're ready to see my lab?"

I nodded. "Yeah, let's do it."

He motioned for me to join him on the other side of the room, just like yesterday. He activated the device, and a moment later the empty classroom disappeared in another blinding flash of light. I remember the feeling well. It was identical to the feeling when he brought us back to 1963, but it went away more quickly, which I was thankful for.

The world came back into focus a few seconds later. I looked around, trying to comprehend what had just happened. It didn't take long for me to realize we really had traveled some 200 miles to Fargo in a matter of seconds. *This is wild,* was all I could remember thinking.

5

As I turned back around, I saw I was standing in front of a stunning house on the corner of a roundabout. Its exterior was almost entirely black with red accents giving the house a clean and modern appearance. We were facing the front entry, which was dominated by quite possibly the largest door I'd ever seen. As we approached the door, I heard a number of what sounded like gears turning, followed by two audible clicks and the opening of the door.

"Well, that sure is convenient," I said, following James inside. "This is a nice place you have." The entry came into the living room and kitchen, both of which were indeed quite nice, but nothing to write home about. There was a single stairwell leading downstairs, and off to the right was the master bedroom.

"Thanks," he said, pointing towards the stairs. "My lab is downstairs. Come on."

I followed him downstairs, unsure of what to expect. In my head I was picturing a small makeshift lab that he had converted his basement into. How silly of me. I don't think my brain could have ever imagined what I was about to walk into—not in a dozen lifetimes.

At the foot of the stairs the floor changed to cement, which made for a jarring last step from the carpet I had been on previously. Fortunately, or maybe unfortunately, this feeling was quickly replaced by the sudden appearance of a massive wall made of some sort of matte colored metal. It actually reminded me of the device James had used to teleport us here.

As I looked around, confused as to where the lab was, a holographic woman appeared in front of the wall.

The hologram was only of her face. She looked to be in her early to mid thirties with shoulder-length wavy brown hair. That was all I could discern of her features due to the partial transparency of her image. She smiled at our presence.

"Welcome back, Dr. Kern," the woman said. "Hello, Andrew Lawson. I hope your trip was okay."

I remember feeling a shiver run through my body at the mention of my name. *How does this holograph know who I am?* Before my brain had time to even begin processing what was happening, the wall (which I now realize was a massive door) began to split in the middle, revealing an impossibly large room. I was frozen in place, but managed to get my legs working as I followed James inside.

"Welcome to my lab, Andrew," he said. The floor once again changed, this time to glass. As we walked farther into the room, lights lit up automatically, further revealing its absurd size.

"Th—thanks," I managed to say. "This is incredible." The holograph appeared in front of us again, causing me to jump backwards.

"My apologies," she said. "I did not mean to startle you."

"This is Anansi," said James, walking over to my side. "She's the AI who runs my house and lab."

"Ni—nice to meet you," I said. "James, what does all of this have to do with the Titanic? With me?"

He walked over to a large l-shaped desk, which held up two large monitors that were connected to a computer tower on the floor. As he sat down, the monitors came to life. A few keystrokes later and I saw a large projection appear in front of us, which seemed to mirror what was on his monitors.

"A few months ago I was working on some tweaks to the Anode Reactor. Due to the complexities that go along with time travel, it takes a great deal of maintenance to keep it working accurately and safely."

He typed a few more things on his keyword, and on the projection appeared a wall of text that could have been English, but it might as well have been hieroglyphics. *This guy is a genius for sure. I heard the AI address him as Dr Kern. I wonder what his doctorate is in?*

"Anyway, while I was running a few tests on it, I accidentally created a wormhole to an alternate timeline."

"I hate when that happens," I said, making a *head-exploding* motion.

James laughed. "Point taken. I could explain the inner workings of wormholes and time travel to you, but it isn't at all relevant that you know how they work... unless you'd like to know, of course. I'd be happy to—"

I held up a hand. "If I don't need to know it, all the better. Besides, I don't think my history teaching brain could handle whatever it is you're doing here."

Another few keystrokes brought up an image of (what I assumed, anyway) was the wormhole. It reminded me of a horizontal tornado—that's the best way I can describe it. In my defense, my brain was doing its best not to implode from everything James had been dropping on me.

"In layman's terms, a wormhole is a tunnel that connects two different points in spacetime. It's primarily how the Anode Reactor works to make time travel possible. Make sense?"

It did, surprisingly. But at the same time, I wasn't too surprised. What's that saying? Something about if you can't explain it simply, you don't understand it well enough?

Regardless, what he was saying made sense, but I still didn't know how it related to the Titanic.

"I'm following, James, but how is this relevant?" I realized how impatient that had sounded. "Sorry, that came out wrong."

He waved a hand as if to say *don't worry about it.*

"It's okay, Andrew, I understand. I have a tendency to get carried away with things like this. I'll get to the point. After creating the wormhole, I had Anansi do some analysis on it, and she discovered it led to an alternate timeline.

"While I have access to a vast amount of computing power, only so much analysis can be done from this side of things. So, I recorded the specific coordinates in spacetime for both ends of the wormhole in the Anode Reactor, and set out to further discover what mysteries this timeline held."

I remember thinking to myself how much courage it must have taken to do something like that. Sure, he knows more about this time travel stuff than I could ever dream of (or would want to), but the idea of heading down a wormhole destined for some alternate timeline terrified the bejesus out of me. But based on what I had heard, I had a pretty good idea of what was different about this timeline—Titanic didn't sink.

"Well, what'd you find out?" I asked.

He smiled. "I'm sure you can guess at least one thing… Titanic indeed hadn't sank in this timeline. I never took the time to figure out why or what happened differently, but there was something else I discovered… it was the something that brought me to you."

James knew how to hook you, that was for sure. I felt the need to know everything about what he discovered. Maybe it was just the history teacher in me, but regardless, I urged him to keep talking.

"Thanks to the Anode Reactor, I was able to cover a significant amount of ground, exploring this new world. It didn't take long to notice the absence of hospitals, nursing homes, or clinics. Instead, I saw a number of medical buildings with the name *Cillian Nanotechnologies* on them. I had Anansi do a bit of digging on the company, and I must say it made for some interesting reading."

The image of the wormhole was replaced with the research on *Cillian Nanotechnologies*, which turned out to have been founded by Cillian Hughes, an Irish scientist who had come to America in 1912—the year wasn't lost on me. Apparently this company specialized in medical nanobots, which had been a revolutionary discovery. These nanobots, James explained, were capable of entering the body and wiping out any and all ailments that were present in the host. This apparently included the flu, pneumonia, and even cancer—from lung to colon. James went on to explain that (no surprise here) Cillian was a passenger on none other than the Titanic. It was at this point that I began to understand what was being asked of me.

"So, you want me to save Cillian, not the Titanic. Right?"

He shook his head. "I don't believe one can be done without the other."

"What? Why not just coax him into not taking that particular voyage? Surely there will be other ships that cross the Atlantic to America."

"In theory that would work, yes. Unfortunately, time travel isn't that easy. The butterfly effect will play against us here, Andrew. Say you do go back and stop him from boarding the

Titanic. You save his life, sure, but we'd have no guarantee he'd ever go to America on another ship."

I realized he was right, of course. Not sure why I thought to question this man in the first place—I was light-years (pun intended there) out of my comfort zone.

"I'm starting to understand," I said, scratching at the back of my neck. "So, I go back to 1912, board the Titanic, find a way to stop it from hitting the iceberg, and then get the two of us back to this time?"

James thought about this for a moment but shook his head again. "No, in order for this to work, meaning we not only save Cillian's life but also ensure he still makes his nanotechnology breakthrough, we need to save the Titanic with him being none the wiser. This last piece is very important. You can't have any contact with him. If you do, even if it's just a casual conversation, the butterfly effect could ruin our whole plan. Does that make sense? Just do whatever it takes to stop the Titanic from sinking and then get yourself out of there."

I sat at the table, lost in my own thoughts, trying to comprehend the conversation that had just taken place. We were talking about traveling back to 1912 and preventing the Titanic from sinking—not exactly small talk over a cup of tea. While that was plenty, the question I kept coming back to was—why me?

I had to know.

"Still with me, Andrew? Does that make sense? This is important."

I nodded. "Yes, sorry. That all makes sense, but what I still don't understand is why you chose me. Sure, I have an obsession with the ship, and I wrote a book about it, but surely that alone doesn't qualify me above the rest of the world for something like this. So, what's the deal?"

James, who was clearly prepared for this very question, responded with little delay.

"I had Anansi do a wide search of the internet in an effort to find any and all teachers who were covering the Titanic in their curriculums. You may or may not be surprised to hear that a search like that brings back a little over 6,000 results. This was obviously no good, so I had her limit it to those teachers who had written a novel on Titanic. This helped, but I was still left with a few hundred results."

Again, at the moment I didn't think anything of this, but now that I'm contemplating it with a different perspective, I can't believe I didn't realize just how creepy this was. Perhaps it was how calm and friendly James was, or maybe it was the possibility of seeing Titanic in person. Either way, this crazy smart scientist had done a lot of work to land on me for this mission.

"So, that got you to a few hundred," I said. "How did I rise to the top of that list? I didn't even think my novel was all that great."

He sighed. "I'll be honest, I'm not proud of this last bit, Andrew. It's… dark, I guess you'd say. Are you sure you want to hear it? I will tell you if you really want to know."

Well now I do, I thought. *Man, this guy should write suspense novels.*

"Tell me."

Another sigh, this one deeper. "Ultimately, I chose you because of who you are."

"I don't follow."

"You're a teacher in an isolated small town. You don't have a girlfriend, wife, or kids. Your family has all sadly passed away." He stopped, likely due to the realization plastered on my face.

"I'm someone that is unlikely to be missed. That's it, right?"

He nodded. "I told you I'm not proud of it. And you can still say no, Andrew. I'd never try to force you to do something you don't want to... especially something as risky as this."

I could tell he meant it. There was pure kindness in his eyes, but there was also shame. He really did feel bad about the reason he chose me. But, to be honest, I couldn't say I blamed him. From a logical standpoint, it made perfect sense. Even if it did hurt a bit to hear, I really was the ideal choice for a mission like this—and that's what I told him.

"I get it, James, I do. I'd be lying if I said hearing it didn't hurt, but ultimately I am the logical choice. I'm still in."

A half smile returned to his face. "Good... great! I'm sorry again that you had to hear that, but I didn't want to lie to you."

"It's okay, James. I understand."

And just like that, we had the makings of a plan. A history teacher from RHS was going to, and pardon this pun, make history by preventing one of the worst maritime disasters of all time. If I succeeded, Cillian Hughes would (we hoped) go on to invent his nanotechnology and rid the world of the many diseases we suffer from today. It sounded too good to be true, but given the rare opportunity I was presented, I had to try.

"I think that's as close to a plan as we're going to get right now," said James. "Let's get you back to Redfield so you can rest and prepare yourself for what's to come. I'll reach out to you in a few days. I have some additional prep work I need to do prior to proceeding."

A flash of light brought me back to the same empty classroom I had met the doctor in a few moments ago. I looked at the clock on the wall, and according to it, our original conversation had just finished.

Time is weird, I thought.

CHAPTER III

1

It was three days after our conversation that I found myself back at James's lab in Fargo. Not unlike my initial reaction to the place, I was again in awe of all the technology running it. Once you got over the shock of Anansi greeting you at the door, the vast room opened up to reveal a glass floor covering an immense server room, which was the heart of the lab.

The two of us sat down at a round desk to discuss our plan in further detail. After all, we weren't just planning a summer road trip or something. This was going to be the biggest event of our lives—the most important one, too. James took out a metal container and placed it in the center of the table.

"Please place your cell phone, wallet, and any other electronics you may have on your person in this container. I will make sure they are returned if you make it back."

While being very well aware of his choice to use 'if' instead of 'when', I did as instructed, only having my phone and wallet to surrender. While I wasn't super attached to my devices, it was an odd feeling to be going without them for an extended period of time. And where I was going, people could only dream of the sophisticated technology that we take for granted in the twenty-first century.

After closing the container, James got up and stored it in a safe that had appeared from a hidden wall behind us. He proceeded to tap on another section of the wall, revealing what looked like a closet, and walked inside. A moment later he reappeared with two brown leather suitcases—old suitcases. Well, old to me, but they would be right at home in 1912.

"You need to look the part," said James, handing me the suitcases. "There is a spare room upstairs you can change in. Feel free to pick your favorite outfit. Although, it's likely none of them are your style. They should be your size, though."

After getting changed, I sat back down at the table with James. The outfits were indeed not my style, but I have to say they were appropriate for the time period. I was now wearing a brown three-piece suit, which felt great. The fit was astonishingly bespoke to my frame, but at the time I didn't consider how weird this was.

James whistled. "You sure clean up nicely." He chuckled before getting back to business. He passed me a manilla envelope across the table, labeled with my name. "Inside you'll find an ID card, your boarding pass, and $50,000 of 1912 currency. While I don't think there will be much use for it while you're onboard, I want you to be prepared."

"Well, you've certainly done that. It must have taken quite a long time to put all this together. How long have you been planning this? Do I want to know?"

He smirked. "Long enough, let's leave it at that. But, like I said, I just want you to be prepared for as many potential scenarios as possible. So, what questions do you have for me? I know I've dropped a lot on you in a short amount of time."

Honestly, I had hundreds of questions. I was a history teacher with an obsession with the Titanic—how could I not? But more so, I just wanted to get on with it and see her for real. Even while I was sitting at the table, I still didn't believe that would ever actually happen. It was just too far-fetched for my poor brain to comprehend.

I shook my head. "I don't think so… just excited, well maybe anxious, to actually see her." As I took another look at my 1912 ID, something came to mind. "What's my plan? How exactly am I going to prevent the ship from sinking?"

"Unfortunately, this is one of the scenarios I am not able to prepare you for. There are just too many variables." He stood up and started to pace around the table. "My best advice would be to take some time to get familiar with your surroundings, talk to people, and try not to draw any unnecessary attention to yourself. Your boarding pass is for first class, so you shouldn't have any issues with accessing most areas of the ship. And don't forget what I said about Cillian… avoid him at all costs. It's a big ship, so I wouldn't think this would be a problem, but we can't afford to not be overly cautious."

I remember sitting at the table, staring unbelievably at my first class ticket for Titanic. I had looked at hundreds of images online of these tickets, always dreaming of what it'd be like to actually have one but knowing I never would. Yet, here I was. Throughout this adventure, I lost count of how many times I thought for sure I was in a vivid dream.

"Understood. So, when do I leave?" I asked, my eagerness getting the better of me.

James smiled. "Whenever you're ready. I imagine you're beside yourself."

I nodded. "I've never been so excited and nervous about something in my life. You should feel my heart rate right now."

"Oh, I almost forgot," said James, reaching into a pocket of the jacket he was wearing. He brought out a very official looking badge wrapped in leather and handed it to me. "The most important thing I have for you."

The badge looked like a driver's license in that it had my name and a small picture of me in the top-right corner. What I noted first, however, was the White Star Line logo that occupied the background of the badge. Under my name was what I assumed to be a title, *Master Engineer,* typed in a bold font. And below that was the following statement:

To whom it may concern, the holder of this card has been appointed to the position of Master Engineer by Her Majesty, The Queen, and is hereby granted unrestricted access to any and all vessels sailing under the British flag. Failure to comply is considered an act of insubordination to the crown and shall be punished accordingly.

"I don't understand," I said, looking back and forth between the badge and James. "I'm not an engineer at all, let alone a *master* engineer, whatever that is. I'm not even British."

James smiled. "Correct. And in 2019, there's no chance that badge would work. But, things were very different in 1912, as I'm sure you can imagine. Back then, if you could talk and act the part, you could pass yourself off as almost anyone or anything." I immediately understood his plan. "With your extensive knowledge of Titanic and all things related, I believe you'll easily be able to pass as a master engineer."

It was a genius plan, really. Having this sort of unrestricted access would make my mission infinitely easier—at least in theory. At the time I still had a hard time believing they'd take the word of some badge with text on it, but again, 1912 was a very different time. I just had to trust James.

"I understand. If this works, it'll make things much easier." I put the badge around my neck.

"Come on," said James, "let's get you on your way."

As I stood on the platform specifically created for this trip, the true reality hit me in a massive wave of emotions. *I'm a history teacher who loves the Titanic, and in a moment I'll get to see her with my own eyes.* My brain still wouldn't let me believe this fact, nevertheless, it really was about to happen. The platform was constructed of a very strong metal, Pruecium I believe, which was the same material used in the Anode Reactor.

"Okay, got everything?"

I nodded. "I think so. Oh, uh… you can bring me back, right? You're sure?"

Can't blame me for asking, can you?

"Rest assured, Andrew, I promise I can bring you back. It's not advisable to return from such a long trip back in time so soon, however, so I'd want you to spend a minimum of twenty-four hours in 1912. If something goes wrong before that time, you'll have to make it work."

Most reassuring.

"What happens if you bring me back before the twenty-four hours are up?"

"The human body isn't designed to experience such drastic changes in space-time without time in-between to regulate itself. You'll start to experience memory lapses, chronic headaches, blurred vision, and then things get really bad."

"Those aren't bad?" A bit of doubt was starting to creep

into my mind. I desperately wanted to see the Titanic, but James wasn't really doing a great job of selling the time travel bit.

"What you have to understand is, this effect I'm talking about scales with how far back in time you go. So, our little trip back to 1963 for example. We only went back fifty-six years. You won't notice anything from that. To get to Titanic, we're talking 107 years. And I know what you're thinking, that's only about double, but time travel is more complicated than that.

"The farther back I ask the AR to send you back, the more power is required to create a larger wormhole, which in turn increases the level of spacetime distortion, causing more severe side-effects on the human body. In order to compensate for this, the person needs to remain in a fixed point in space-time to allow the effects of this distortion to dissipate."

Part of me was sorry I asked. I felt my brain beginning to swell. But, at the same time I was thankful for his honesty.

"I think I understand. So, ideally I'll be back there for four days, which will be fine, right?"

"Yup, four days is more than enough time to compensate for the distortion. You won't experience any side-effects, save for some nausea when you get there and come back."

"Okay, got it. Let's do this. Oh, wait.. where will I end up? Southampton?"

He nodded. "Yes, sir. April 10th, 1912. The launch time was roughly at noon, with passengers boarding between nine thirty and eleven, so I'm sending you there at nine. This should give you enough time to orient yourself and get on the ship."

"I'm not going to suddenly appear in the middle of a busy street or something, right?" I should have known better, considering how well prepared James had been so far, but I needed to hear it for myself.

"Of course not. The coordinates I have programmed into the AR will place you on Albert Rd. It's about half a mile north of the docks, which will be far enough away for you to avoid the crowds of the upcoming launch."

James typed out a few commands on his keyboard and then turned on the AR, presenting me with that short high-pitched hum before going silent. He walked up to the platform, standing five feet in front of me, and held out the device.

"Okay, everything is good to go. Thank you in advance for your efforts. I've done all I can to prepare you for your journey, and I think with your knowledge of the ship, you'll be able to handle anything that may come up."

A last minute question came to me. "How will you know I am ready to come back? Or… if I am even still alive?" I didn't like the thought of either of these questions, but I knew they needed to be asked.

"Oh, right… sorry," he said, pointing to his head. "the old brain isn't what it used to be."

If this was his brain being "old", it's hard to imagine him in his prime.

"Anyway, in one of your suitcases is a small pair of earpieces. Once you're ready to go, or something comes up and you need to talk to me, put them in your ear and they'll activate. But, please reserve this for emergencies. The amount of power it takes to communicate across a wormhole is immense. Understood?"

Frankly, I couldn't imagine how much power it would take to do anything across a wormhole—I couldn't even imagine what a wormhole was, for that matter. Regardless, my brain heard that James had a way for us to communicate in an emergency, and that was good enough for me.

"Has anyone ever told you you're too smart for your own good?"

James laughed. "More than a few times, but I do my best to stay humble about it. I just want to help when I can. Anyway, shall we?" I nodded and took hold of my bags. "Good luck, Andrew. Safe travels. Oh, and have a go at the Turkish bath for me, will you? I hear it was quite an experience."

Before I could respond, James initiated the AR, and in a flash of brilliant light the lab disappeared. Like before, I felt my body and mind separating, which was something I could have lived without feeling ever again. Thankfully, this was short-lived, and a moment later I felt a cool sensation on my face. Next thing I knew, my surroundings came into full view—I was on a patch of grass, hidden from a nearby road (presumably Albert Rd).

I took a quick look around to get a feel for my surroundings. It was an overcast sky, and the morning was cool. The next thing I quickly took note of was the quality of the air—it was appalling. This wasn't surprising, especially considering my current proximity to the docks. Large numbers of boats, all coal burning, passing through at all hours of the day. A smile came over my face. Despite the likely toxic levels of CO2 in the air, the history teacher in me was elated at the prospect of things to come.

I was most certainly in the past. I clapped my hands together and laughed. *James is crazy, no question about it, but he is a genius. He actually figured out time travel.* To this day I still marvel at the thought.

I looked at my watch—9:04. Twenty-six minutes until

passengers would begin boarding Titanic. I felt another wave of excitement rush through my body. *I have to see her.* I picked up my suitcases and began a brisk walk to the docks.

Titanic awaits!

2

RMS Titanic, a British registered ocean liner, was designed and constructed at the Harland & Wolff shipyard in Belfast (Yard No. 401), Northern Ireland. Due to the sheer size of her, the shipyard's docks had to be completely rebuilt to accommodate such an undertaking. Beginning in 1909, it would take three years to complete the construction, with several setbacks along the way—including the process grinding to a halt when her sister ship, Olympic, needed to be suddenly repaired after colliding with another vessel.

When completed, Titanic had an overall length of 882 feet, 9 inches, a height of 175 feet (measured from the top of the funnels to the keel), and a gross tonnage of 46, 328 tons. Needless to say, she was a colossal structure—the largest ship in existence at the time. She was praised as being 'unsinkable', and promised to offer the most luxurious experience money could buy. But, as we all know, four short days after setting sail from Southampton, she would strike an iceberg and sink in just under three hours.

The wreck of Titanic wouldn't be discovered until 1985 (more than seventy years after the disaster) by Robert Ballard. Prior to this, it was long thought that the ship sank in one piece, when in fact it had broken in two prior to plunging to the Atlantic's depths. She still holds the record as the largest cruise liner to ever sink. Not exactly the kind of record you'd like to hold, but it's one that she holds nevertheless.

The Titanic rests at the bottom of the Atlantic, 2.4 miles down from the surface. Her bow and stern section are separated by approximately 650 yards, between which are countless pieces of debris from the sinking. While the stern suffered significant structural damages on its way down, the bow was mostly intact until it plunged itself sixty feet into the seafloor.

Since the initial discovery in 1985, numerous expeditions have been made to the wreck site, salvaging over 5,500 objects from the ship. The biggest of which was a 17-ton section of the hull, recovered in 1997. Many of these recovered items are part of several traveling Titanic museums, however, a permanent museum in Missouri holds over 400 of the recovered objects.

3

It was 9:16 a.m. I'd remember that point in time for the rest of my life. It was when I first arrived at Berth 44—Titanic's berth. Even as I write this now, thinking back to that cool April morning in 1912, the image of her awaiting to take on passengers is as clear as ever. From the bustling noise of all the people hauling their luggage towards the dock, to the endless cawing of seagulls, to the smell of salt from the sea and the burning coal from the ships, the scene was as surreal as I thought it would be. I often reminisce about seeing her for the first time.

Titanic—at the time, was the largest ship in the world. As I approached her, I had to bend my neck nearly as far back as I could to take it all in. The utter size of the ship, docked in her berth, is difficult to put into words. Throughout my years of research I had seen hundreds of pictures of her at this very spot, however, not one of them even came close to conveying her scale.

I smiled—smiled so much my face would hurt for hours afterward.

I looked down at my watch, which now said 9:24—just six more minutes until passengers would be starting to board. *I should get in line,* I thought. I wanted to be one of the first onboard.

A moment later, I was waiting to walk across the boarding ramp and onto D Deck. It took everything I had to control myself. I was soon to be inside the most famous ocean liner in maritime history. The line of people began to move, and when it was finally my turn I managed to compose myself long enough to show the officer my ticket. He nodded, and then I was through.

I was onboard the Titanic.

Thanks to James, I had the pleasure of staying in a first class cabin. Cabin C-73. After boarding on D deck, I went up one level, which gave me my first look at the magnificent Grand Staircase. Like everything about the Titanic, the scale of it was something to be admired. Running from the Boat Deck down to D Deck, it was one of the most notable pieces of the ship—even after 107 years. I'd looked at countless photos of the oak stairs, and even saying they don't do the real thing justice would be an understatement in itself. They were nothing short of breathtaking.

I can confidently say that walking up the Grand Staircase for the first time was one of the highlights of my life. After all the years of only seeing it in photos, actually being able to touch it caused me to get a little emotional. To some that may sound silly—it's just a staircase, after all. But, those who say that simply don't understand. At the time, this was the peak of architecture and style—nothing up to that point could even compare to her level of luxury. And on top of all that, being the Titanic enthusiast that I was, this experience made for quite a dramatic start to my time onboard.

Cabin C-73 was on Titanic's Starboard side. After walking up the Grand Staircase to C Deck I headed aft towards the stern. I couldn't help but notice how new everything looked and smelled. I was, in fact, one of the very first people to step foot into any of these rooms. A moment later, I found myself standing in front of the door to my cabin. *Time to see it with my own eyes.*

Like in the hallway, as I stepped into my room I was greeted by the smell of fresh paint. Immediately to the left of the door was my double bed, its head and foot adorned with beautiful filigree. Across from it was a small dining table set for two. Towards the end of the room were both a floor to ceiling wardrobe and the most over-the-top vanity I'd ever seen. The top of it was constructed of beautiful white marble, with the bottom being cherry oak—the contrast was stunning.

As I continued farther inside, my feet felt the plushness of the carpet, which was a deep blue with a repeating white star pattern. I sat my suitcase down next to the wardrobe and took a seat on the sofa next to it. *I'm in a first class cabin on the Titanic*, I remember thinking. Dreams really do come true. After a few more blissful moments of taking in my surroundings, I figured it was time to get going. I had plenty of work to do, and unfortunately for both me and the ship, not a lot of time.

I stood up and looked at my reflection in the mirror, almost not recognizing myself in the lavish bespoke suit I was currently wearing. That said, I really did look the part—James had done a phenomenal job with the attire. And the flat cap adorned on my head was the quintessential cherry on top. I looked like a proper gentleman.

A knock at the door startled me out of my reverie. *Who could that be?* I got up and cautiously opened the door.

"Good morning, sir," said a man in a black suit with a white undershirt. "I am Smethells, your steward." *Ah yes, I forgot. First class passengers have their own steward.* "Is everything in order with your cabin, sir?"

I nod. "Yes, yes it's great. I'm Andrew by the way, Andrew Lawson." I put out my hand. I don't think he was expecting such a gesture, and I should have known better, but he smiled and shook my hand nevertheless.

"Nice to meet you, sir. Will you be needing any assistance from me at the moment?"

"I think I'm good for now, thank you."

"Very good, sir. If you do need something, please use the buzzer next to your door. I am available at all hours of the day and night. Enjoy your day. We'll be departing soon." And with that he left, closing the door behind him.

Alone again, it was time for me to explore Titanic.

4

Upon leaving my cabin, I wandered back to the grand staircase and made my way up to the Boat Deck. Just as I reached A Deck I noticed a familiar man. With his neat black hair, bits of grey throughout and an always friendly expression on his face, Thomas Andrews was most recognizable—particularly to a history buff such as myself.

Born in 1873, the thirty-nine-year-old was the chief designer of Titanic, and knew every nook and cranny of the ship. All the articles written about the disaster speak highly of

Andrews, saying he saved as many people as he could before the ship went down. A steward, supposedly the last person to see him that night, reported he saw the designer staring off into space near a painting in the first class smoking room.

I briefly waved at him. "Mr. Andrews? Is that you?" While I of course knew it was, I felt in the moment it was better for him to think I was unsure.

The friendly expression never left his face as he nodded. "Most certainly, sir. And to whom may I ask, am I speaking?" He offered his hand.

"Andrew Lawson," I said, taking his hand in mine.

He looked down and saw my badge, quickly skimming over it. I saw his face acknowledge the truth, giving away his excitement.

"Oh my," he said. "A master engineer on Titanic's maiden voyage. Splendid!" He took his other hand and put it over mine, still enveloped in our handshake. "It is an honor, sir."

I smiled, my excitement equally as high to meet him. "It's an honor to meet you as well, sir. I admire the work you've done on the ship. She's incredible." I motioned towards the staircase of A Deck. "And this, this is just breathtaking."

"Well, thank you very much. A master engineer who admires my work? Never thought I'd see the day, to be honest." The smile now on his face was the most genuine I'd ever seen. I knew he was a humble man, especially for the time period, but I was taken aback by it at that moment. "It really is nice to meet you, Mr. Lawson and I'd love to chat with you more about Titanic, but you caught me on my way to see Captain Smith. Shall we meet in the smoking room, say just after we set sail? One p.m.?"

"Oh, my apologies, Mr. Andrews. Please forgive the intrusion. I shouldn't have just walked up to you like I did." I knew he wouldn't have taken this encounter as an intrusion, but I couldn't help but apologize. It's just how I was.

He put up a hand. "No apology needed, Mr. Lawson, I assure you. See you at one then?"

"Yes, of course! It would be my pleasure."

He smiled and nodded, starting to walk off. "The pleasure will be all mine."

And that was my first interaction with the legendary ship designer, Thomas Andrews. It was hard to stand and talk to him knowing what I knew. In just four days, all of this would be at the bottom of the Atlantic, and 1,500 people would parish in the icy waters. As I stood there replaying my conversation with Andrews, looking around at the beautiful craftsmanship of the ship, I knew there was no way I could ruin this chance to save her. No matter what it took, I was going to stop the Titanic from hitting that iceberg.

CHAPTER IV

1

It was twelve p.m. on April 10th, 1912 when Titanic set sail on her maiden voyage from Southampton. With 2,208 on board (1,317 passengers and 891 crew members), she was the start to a new (and hopefully) better life for many. She would make two more stops—Cherbourg, France and Queenstown, Ireland (now known as Cobh)—afterward continuing out into the Atlantic, making her fated journey to New York.

After my brief but glorious interaction with Mr. Andrews, I made my way up to the Boat Deck to look around while waiting for us to depart. As I exited the staircase on the port side, one thing immediately stuck out to me—the view wasn't cluttered.

Back in the early days of Titanic's design, Alexander Carlisle, who at the time was Harland & Wolff's chief draftsman and manager, submitted a plan for her to have sixty-four lifeboats. Later this was halved, and then in March 1910 it was taken down to twenty. It's rumored that this decision was due to the fact that the additional lifeboats would make the Boat Deck too cluttered, however, the most agreed upon reasoning behind this was that she was seen as a lifeboat herself—she was seen as unsinkable.

I walked aft a couple feet and stood at the railing, looking at the crowd of excited onlookers below. A moment later, I saw two tugboats approach, readying themselves to push Titanic out of her berth. I joined the hundreds of other passengers in waving at the people on the dock as we slowly moved away from them and out to open water. Now that her maiden voyage was officially underway, the clock was ticking.

I had four days to prevent a maritime disaster.

2

Titanic's first class smoking room was designed to emulate the cozy affluence of a gentleman's club. It was lined with ornate and intricately carved mahogany paneling, as well as hand-painted stained glass windows. As I walked inside, I was immediately greeted by the overwhelming smell of cigar smoke. Not surprising given the name, but it still caught me off guard, especially since I wasn't a smoker.

It didn't take long to spot Andrews, who was sitting at a small table in the corner. He saw me almost at the same time and waved me over.

"Hello again, Mr. Lawson," he said, motioning for me to take a seat. "What do you think of her so far?"

I pulled out the burgundy leather chair and sat down, quickly noticing the luxurious feel of it as it enveloped my body. *I could get used to this,* I thought.

"She's quite a ship," I said, still finding it hard to believe this was happening. "Thanks for meeting with me, sir. I really do appreciate it."

He smiled and took a sip of his drink. "It is my pleasure, really. Say, would you care for something to drink? We have anything you could ever want, just name it."

I shook my head. "Maybe later, but thank you."

"Suit yourself. So, a master engineer onboard for Titanic's maiden voyage. To what do we owe the pleasure? Reporting back to the crown on White Star's latest and greatest I assume?"

This was my primary reason for not accepting a drink. I knew I was a lightweight when it came to alcohol, and I needed to keep my mind clear. I couldn't let something slip that would give myself away. While it may come to a point where I have to do just that, I wanted to play it safe as long as I could.

"Nothing official, sir. This is primarily a personal journey. I've been looking forward to these new Olympic-class liners for quite some time. I wasn't around for the Olympic's maiden voyage, so I made sure I didn't miss Titanic's. But, while I'm here, if I do happen to notice anything, good or bad, I'll be sure to make a note of it."

He smiled. "Of that I have no doubt, Mr. Lawson."

I glanced around at my surroundings, taking in the intricate designs on the ceiling and walls. There really was so much to admire about the ship. "I must say, it's been quite an experience for me already, being onboard this luxurious ship. You've done a great job."

"Well, thank you very much, Mr. Lawson."

"Please," I said, "call me Andrew."

"Andrew it is. You may call me Thomas if you'd like. So,

what do you find yourself liking the most about Titanic? Surely there's something."

I'm sure you'll get tired of me saying this (if you haven't already), but I can't stress enough how surreal it was for me to be aboard the Titanic. Not just that, but sitting in the smoking room with her chief designer. I was like a kid in a candy story that stocked all of your favorite candy—and also the candy was free. I was borderline giddy at the thought of it all, so you can imagine how difficult it was for me to formulate complete sentences, but I somehow managed to do so.

"There really is so much to like," I said. "I'll admit I was taken aback when I first saw the scale of her at the dock. I had gotten some early glimpses of her during construction, but the finished product is quite remarkable."

He nodded and took another drink, "Her scale is like nothing ever built by man. And she's still able to achieve a speed of twenty-three knots."

The mention of speed made me wince, but I'm hoping he didn't notice. One of the primary contributors to her hitting the iceberg was her speed at the time—which was reported to be 22.5 knots. The night of the disaster, seven ice warnings were received (six of which would reach Captain Smith). The truth may never be discovered as to why the Captain ignored them, but the leading theory is they simply believed anything large enough to hurt the ship would be seen in time.

I decided at that point to take a risk. Everything I'd read about Andrews said he argued passionately about the number of lifeboats onboard. I wanted to hear it from him.

"Can I ask you about something?"

He took another quick drink, emptying his glass. "I'd be disappointed if you didn't." Another smile formed on his face.

I pretty much knew the answer to my question already. This man was one of the good ones.

"I heard the number of lifeboats was cut back significantly. Something about them making the Boat Deck look cluttered? Or was it because the ship was seen as a lifeboat herself?"

His smile faltered for the first time that afternoon. "You hear a lot, Andrew. It's true, the original number was sixty-four. It was cut to thirty-two, and then to twenty. While I can understand not wanting to always see them while on the Boat Deck, I personally feel not having enough lifeboats for all passengers and crew onboard is irresponsible at best, and utter negligence at worst."

And there it was—history was right. I could have asked him more, but I thought I knew the rest. He fought to get forty-eight lifeboats, but nobody would hear it. At the time, the Board of Trades deemed twenty lifeboats to be enough for Titanic, and so that is how many she would have—end of story. He even argued that the ship should have a double walled hull as well as watertight bulkheads that extended to B Deck as opposed to only E Deck. If only the people who over-ruled him knew how much they were handicapping the ship by doing so. Hindsight being twenty twenty and all that.

Thomas took out a pocket watch and stood up from his chair. "Do forgive me, Andrew, but I must be going. Let's have a drink together sometime on the trip. Come find me in my cabin if you're feeling up for it. A-36." He shook my hand and made his way out of the room.

After taking a moment to come down from my high of getting to chat with Thomas Andrews, I decided I should get to work on my 'mission', for lack of a better word. I needed a place to think.

3

I decided getting a cup of coffee in the Café Parisien, located on B Deck, would be the perfect place to think. It was promoted as a replica of a Parisian sidewalk café, hence the name. With its stark white trellises, covered in live ivy, and a green carpet running the length of the room, it always seemed like a quirky place to me—one I wanted to see.

It was just after two when I sat down in the cafe. There were a few other passengers, but it was still pretty quiet. From my understanding, this area of the ship wasn't commonly used. I asked for a cup of black coffee, and a moment later it was on the table in front of me, poured in fine china.

As I sipped my coffee, I took a moment to reflect on my situation. It was only 2:24 p.m. on the first day of the voyage, so I still had time. That being said, given the circumstances, and knowing what would happen if I fail (Titanic sinks), I wasn't about to become complacent. I made a mental note of Mr Andrews's invitation to have a drink with him sometime in his cabin. I had a feeling he would be one of my primary contacts while I was onboard. *Perhaps he can help.*

I spent another thirty minutes enjoying the view out the windows of the cafe while having a second cup of coffee. During that time I met two other passengers doing the same thing. Mr. and Mrs. William Baxter. Will, which he insisted I call him, was an oil investor who was traveling with his wife, Marge, to America for business. They were pleasant people, and found my interest in the ship to be rather fascinating. We chatted a bit longer about various topics, not much more than small talk, and then I excused myself to return to my cabin.

4

One thing worth noting (there are many) about the sinking of the Titanic is that it was completely and utterly avoidable. Starting back in 1909, before her keel was even laid, her fate had been sealed. The material chosen to make the rivets, which held the ship's hull together, was wrought iron as opposed to steel. This money saving decision meant the rivets would be significantly more brittle when exposed to cold temperatures—you know, such as the icy waters of the Atlantic. Due to this oversight, when Titanic's hull connected with the iceberg, the rivets popped off, allowing water to slip in-between the panels and increase the amount of flooding.

Another well-known strike against her was the excessive speed on the night of the disaster. Despite multiple ice warnings, Titanic still proceeded to cruise along at nearly twenty-three knots. Why? Because not only did White Star want her to be the largest ship ever built, they wanted her to be the fastest. It was their goal to beat the time it took Olympic, her sister ship, to cross the Atlantic. Originally scheduled to get into New York on the afternoon of Wednesday the 17th, Captain Smith was urged to try for Tuesday evening. But of course, that would never happen.

5

I spent the remainder of the afternoon in my cabin, getting my things settled. It was nearly seven when I realized I hadn't eaten anything. Holding a first class ticket, I knew I would have a near endless amount of food options for dinner. I put my shoes and hat back on and made my way down to D Deck, which housed the first class dining saloon. As I approached the ornately decorated French doors, I came upon a woman being escorted towards the lower decks by two officers. She was struggling (to no avail) against the men's grip on her arms.

"I am sorry, miss," said one of the officers. "We simply can't allow unticketed passengers to freely roam the ship. You are to be in custody of the Master-at-Arms until we reach New York."

The woman wore a simple brown skirt and a white blouse, both of which looked to be quite old. Her brown hair, albeit greasy and astray, looked particularly beautiful to me. Her struggling increased as she heard of her fate.

"Please, sir," she pleaded, "don't leave me down there. I haven't eaten in days… I'm so hungry. Can I just have a little bit to eat? I promise I won't be of any more trouble afterward." Tears had started to fall along the side of her face.

I could tell both officers were over the conversation, rolling their eyes and trying to be as discreet as possible to avoid concerning the other passengers. As the woman desperately looked around the hallway, I approached and spoke to the officers.

"Excuse me, officers," I said, waving my hand. They stopped, and the one who had been trying to reason with the woman spoke.

"Apologies for interrupting you on your way to dinner, sir. We'll be taking her down below right away."

"No interruption, but I was wondering about what's going on here."

"Just some official business that needs tak—" His eyes glanced down from mine and landed on my *master engineer* badge. He suddenly stopped leading (borderline dragging by this point) the woman, and his fellow officer stopped as well, following the man's gaze. "Ah, sorry, I didn't know," he said, gesturing towards the badge. "Is there anything we can do for you, sir?"

I pointed to the lady. "Why is she being detained?" I had overheard his comment a moment ago, but I wanted to hear it from him.

He cleared his throat. "She's a stowaway, sir. We caught her just after we had departed Cherbourg. Not sure if that's where she got on or not, but not to worry, we'll make sure she stays put down below."

I thought for a moment and then shook my head. "If it's all the same to you two, I will take custody of her for the duration of our journey." I maintained my composure externally, but on the inside I was freaking out. *They'll call my bluff,* I thought. *They won't buy the whole 'appointed by The Queen' nonsense.*

The two officers looked at each other and then back to me. The one who had been doing the talking shrugged. "Better you than us I suppose." He let go of her and pushed her gently towards me. "Just keep an eye on her, she's escaped our custody twice now."

I smiled, briefly making eye contact with the lady. "I'll keep that in mind. Thank you, officers." They nodded and walked off towards the staircase, clearly thankful to be done with her.

I turned back to her. "Hi, miss."

She turned to face me, and I was greeted by her caramel colored eyes—there was kindness in those eyes, but there was also fear. I imagine she saw my attire and thought for sure I wasn't going to be any better company than the officers.

"I'm sorry, sir," she said, bowing her head. "I don't want any trouble. I'm just hungry…" I'd never seen such fear in someone before. Her head remained down as I slowly approached her and put my hand on her shoulder. She stiffened.

"What's your name?"

There was a pause, but a moment later she raised her head, and I saw her face was filled with confusion. "M—my name?" I nodded. "Hanna, sir. My name is Hanna. Why do you want to know?"

I smiled and put out my arm for her to hook hers in. "How about being my date for dinner, Hanna?"

Her look of confusion deepened, and part of me thought she felt I was trying to get her hopes up. I really wanted her to say yes, though. Not sure what it was, but there was something about her—I wanted to get to know her. As she continued to study my facial expression, she seemed to realize I wasn't kidding.

"Wait, you're serious? You want *me* to join you for dinner? In *there*?" She motioned towards the saloon.

I nod again. "Yes, of course. Would that be okay?"

It took her a moment, but then she smiled, likely for the first time in ages and hooked her arm inside of mine. "Lead the way!"

We walked back across the hall and stopped in front of the door. The steward smiled and nodded to me, but then frowned as he turned to her. I spoke up before he could.

"She's my guest for the evening."

I could tell he wanted to rebut, however, he simply nodded to me again. "Very good, sir." He opened the door and stepped aside. "Do enjoy your meals."

As we walked into the saloon, both of us were taken aback by the sheer size of the room. It was, in fact, the first time either of us had been there. The first class dining saloon was the largest room on the ship. It was 114 ft long and ran the entire width of Titanic. It could accommodate in excess of 500 passengers, and seeing as there were just over 300 first class passengers onboard, its immense size was further made apparent. Lined with wood paneling that was painted a brilliant white, and blue linoleum floors featuring an elaborate red and yellow pattern, it was the pinnacle of dining in luxury.

We found an empty table set for two, isolated from the other passengers, and took our seats. I remember the continued feeling of not belonging—not just this timeline but in first class. I hope this has already been made apparent, but back in 2019 I'm just a regular guy. I teach history, obsess over the Titanic, and have the occasional beer with my friend, John. I was the furthest from first class passenger material you could find. Nevertheless, I planned to enjoy this once in a lifetime opportunity to its fullest.

Not long after we sat down, a waiter dropped off two ornate decorated glasses of ice water along with our menus.

"Good evening," he said, placing our cloth napkins on our laps. It was, as you can imagine, a bit too formal for my liking. "May I get either of you something to drink besides the water?"

"I'll take a bourbon on the rocks," I said, wanting to relax a little.

"Very good, sir. And for you, miss?" It was apparent that she felt out of place as well, likely even more so. While I thought she looked great in her skirt and blouse, it certainly didn't meet the high fashion dress code for first class. Despite this fact, the waiter didn't seem to notice.

"A glass of red wine would be lovely."

"Red wine for the lady, of course," said the waiter, bowing and leaving us to look at our menus.

One thing to note about being in first class, you really

were treated like royalty. Mealtimes were no exception—in fact, it was made even more apparent. For dinner, there could be as many as ten courses—and you were free to order any or all of the items on the menu. Because I wanted to get the true experience, I planned to get one of everything. Call me a pig if you'd like, but after you see what was being offered below, I think you'll understand.

After our waiter returned with our drinks, we ordered our food. Hanna was still a bit overwhelmed at everything, so she agreed to let me order on her behalf.

The first course was a choice of two soups; a consommé rejane, which is a clear soup with a beef broth base, or a créme reine margot, which is a cream-based soup. Second course was turbot or whitebait fish—essentially sardines in a lobster-flavored sauce. Third course was mutton cutlets and green peas or a dish called Supreme of Chicken à la Stanley, which was a fancy way of describing a creamy chicken dish. Apparently "supreme" is a French term, meaning the chicken is boneless and skinless.

At this point, even though I had just been saying yes to everything, I was getting a bit overwhelmed with all of the dish names in front of me, and there were still five courses left to choose. First world problems, right?

The fourth course was a sirloin of beef with château potatoes, roast duckling and apple sauce, or filet of veal and braised ham. The fifth course was (thankfully) a bit lighter—cauliflower and spinach. The sixth course brought boiled rice, bovine, and boiled new potatoes. The seventh course was plover on toast and cress with a salad. Plover is a bird, and cress is an English herb.

The eighth course (dessert number one) was pudding Sans Souci or Charlotte Colville and Granvilles. Sans Souci is a

French term that simply means "no worries". Charlotte Colville was a gelatin dessert and Granvilles a type of cracker. And finally, the ninth course (dessert number two), was French ice cream. I was starving at this point and couldn't wait to dig into all of that food.

Our waiter smiled at us, took the menus, and left us to enjoy our drinks while we waited for the first course. A bit of awkward silence fell between us. I wanted to ask more about her but wasn't sure where to start. After all, we're from two completely different timelines. She beat me to it, however.

"So," she began, taking a sip of her wine. "To what do I owe the pleasure? Mr?"

"Lawson. Andrew Lawson."

"Nice to meet you, Mr. Lawson."

I smiled. "Please, call me Andrew.

"Okay then, Andrew. Why me? Why did you invite me in for dinner? If you're hoping to get personal with me, I won't have it. Just because you're of a higher class doesn't give you the right to take whatever you please. I don't care how many meals you invite me to." She took another sip of wine, the agitation evident in her voice. "And don't think giving me more of this will improve your chances either."

I shook my head and put up my hands in a surrender motion. "Nothing of the kind, Hanna, I assure you. I don't like seeing women, or anyone for that matter, treated like objects just because they aren't as privileged as some. Or if someone is down on their luck and having a rough go at life. We should be helping those in need, not punishing them. I'd just like to get to know you."

I paused to take a drink—the bourbon was of the finest quality, and I was already starting to feel it.

"But, please don't feel pressured to indulge my curiosity. If all that comes of this is some good food and drink, that's just fine with me." I smiled at her and offered my glass for a cheers.

After a moment she returned my smile and our glasses clinked. "Okay then, Mr. Laws… I mean, Andrew, what would you like to know?"

6

Hanna and I spent several hours talking and eating our dinners. She was thirty-four and single, on her way to New York in hopes of a better life. I wasn't surprised. This had been the dreams of many aboard the Titanic. All those dreams, swallowed by the Atlantic Ocean on a cold night in April. *Not if I can help it,* I thought. *Not if I can help it.*

She had asked about me and what I do, to which I told her the same story I had told Mr. Andrews. I was an engineer who was onboard as a regular passenger on the ship's maiden voyage. She had seemed curious about this, and even asked me about a few facts regarding the ship.

As she emptied her fourth glass of wine, her eyes finally noticed my badge. I had forgotten about it, which happened more often than I cared to admit.

Her eyes grew as she read it. "A master engineer appointed by the Queen herself? I'm having dinner with someone appointed by Her Majesty? Something doesn't fit here, Mr. Lawson."

I smile at her. "It's Andrew, remember? And I promise there's no ulterior motive to my actions. Who wants to eat dinner alone?"

I could tell she didn't quite believe me, but she relaxed again, likely helped by the wine. She pointed at my badge.

"So, that's why the officers gave me up so easily. You have the run of this ship, don't you?"

I shrug. "It seems that way, but I'm not one for power or control. Just here to do my job."

The waiter came to our table and asked if we wanted another round. I told him we'd do one more. He bowed and left, shortly returning with bourbon and wine.

"I don't understand you," she said, taking a large gulp of her now full glass of wine. "No man of your class and particular standing would care at all about someone in my position." *Ouch,* I thought. But it was a fair statement for the time period. "Don't get me wrong, this has been lovely, I just don't get it. You say you aren't up to anything, and I'd like to believe you, but surely you must see how odd this is."

I knew how odd it looked. Even in 2019, more often than not people cared more about themselves than others. I disagreed with this mindset, of course, and always tried to help when I could. As a teacher, this kind of empathy and kindness created a better experience for my students. While this kind of behavior was uncommon in 2019, it was downright unheard of in 1912. There was no mixing of classes—it was seen as appalling.

"I can see how others would think it odd," I said. "But, I disagree with the notion of different classes of people not being able to interact."

She seemed like she might be coming around at that point—or maybe it was the wine. Either way, she left the topic alone for the rest of the evening. We talked a little more about this and that, and after another half hour and two more drinks each, we headed out the dining saloon doors and into the hallway.

"Are you ta—taking me back to the officers now?" She was

a little uneasy on her feet, so I steadied her by putting her arm over my shoulder.

"No, you can sleep on the couch in my suite."

After a pause, "I told you no funny business. Do you swear?"

"Scouts honor," I said.

"What?" *Oops,* I thought. Scout's honor won't be a thing for fifty years.

"I swear, no funny business. I just want you to have a safe place to sleep." I felt her lean more into me, accepting my offer in silence.

"Okay," she finally said. "Let's go, I'm tired."

We make our way up the staircase and down the hall to C-73. She takes the couch, as planned, and I fall into my bed, almost passing out immediately.

"Thank you very much for dinner, Andrew. It was a lovely evening."

I smiled. "You're welcome, Hanna. Good night."

"Good night."

CHAPTER V

3 DAYS, 18 HOURS UNTIL DISASTER

1

While my first day on Titanic made me feel like an aforementioned kid in a candy store, it was not particularly productive in terms of figuring out how to stop its impending fate. I knew time wasn't on my side, so I made it a point to start formulating a plan. First and foremost, I had to figure out who (if anyone) I could convince that the ship was actually going to sink. My recent acquaintance, Hanna, came to my mind, but even if she believed me (which was another problem in itself) I didn't think there would be anything she could do.

As James had predicted, the master engineer badge he gave me seemed to be the equivalent of being the Queen herself on this ship. I indeed had full access to any area of the ship, and so far nobody had questioned me in any way. I'm hoping to use this to my advantage, but I was still left with the obvious problem—convincing people that Titanic, the unsinkable ship that redefined luxury and safety at sea, was going to sink in three days.

These thoughts went through my mind as I laid in bed on that Thursday morning. Hanna, who I suspected had a bit too much wine last night, was still fast asleep on the sofa. The throbbing in my head reminded me of my own indulgences from the night before. I realized then how inappropriate it was for me to let her stay in my room, but I couldn't bring myself to give her back to the custody of White Star's officers. She'd just end up back in the decks below, a prisoner until she met her fate in the icy waters of the Atlantic.

As if she heard my thoughts about her, Hanna began to stir on the couch. A moment later she sat up and immediately locked eyes with me. At first, I saw fear, but this was quickly replaced with understanding.

"You kept your word," she said, remembering the events of last night. "Thank you, Andrew. You really are a proper gentleman."

I sat up and put my legs over the side of the bed. "No need to thank me, I just did what was right."

The fear in her eyes returned. "What happens now? Will you release me back to those men? I suppose you will."

I could hear a tremble starting in her voice. Such a shame for someone to be living in fear all the time.

"No," I said. "They released you to my custody for the duration of our trip. But, I plan to do more than that. I'm going to make it known that you're my personal guest on this ship, and you are to be left alone."

Her eyes lit up. "You really mean it? I—I won't have to hide anymore?"

I shook my head. "As it should be. I'm so sorry for how you've been treated."

She looked perplexed. "I still don't get you, Andrew. What kind of man with your high standing takes time out of his day to do something like that?"

I stood up from my bed and walked to the couch, sitting down beside her. I took her hand in mine, which I was surprised to see she didn't hesitate.

"The kind of man who respects women and knows that at the end of the day, class or standing doesn't mean much of anything." A moment later she embraced me in a hug, tears starting to fall down her face.

After a few seconds she let go and looked at me. "I don't know how to thank you, and I doubt I ever will."

I smiled. "There's no need, Hanna." I pulled out my pocket watch and saw it was just after eight. "I better get going. I need to meet with someone to get everything in order for you."

"Just what are you planning to do for me?"

I lifted up my badge. "I'm going to make use of this. You'll see when I get back. I shouldn't be gone more than twenty minutes. In the meantime, feel free to freshen up."

She smiled and hugged me again. "Thank you so much, Andrew."

"Of course, Hanna. I'll be back."

2

Another fact about Titanic's maiden voyage, one that almost ended the trip before it even began, was the near-miss she had with the SS New York. The SS New York was docked at Southampton, like many, due to the coal shortage. As Titanic was leaving port, the suction caused by her gigantic size broke the other ship loose from her hawsers, which she was tied to. As the two ships were imminently on a collision course, two tugboats raced to pull back the other ship while Titanic reversed her engines. Thankfully, all was well and the voyage continued after a brief delay. Despite never actually colliding with the SS New York, many believed the incident to be an ill omen for Titanic's maiden voyage.

One of the bigger issues on Titanic, although not well-known, was the coal fire in one of the bunkers between boiler room #5 and #6. It's believed the fire, which was caused by the use of sub-par coal, had been active while she was still in Belfast. In-between these two bunkers was one of the ship's watertight bulkheads, which had spent the entire maiden voyage (and even before) exposed to this fire, potentially reaching peak temperatures of 1,000 degrees celsius.

This fire created two issues for Titanic, both of which were now thought to have contributed to her fate. The first being the extreme temperatures the watertight bulkhead had been exposed to for nearly eight days. At temperatures above 500 degrees celsius, steel can lose 40 percent or more of its strength. And this is before taking into account the Titanic was built using weaker steel in an effort to save money (supposedly). The steel used had higher sulphur and phosphorus concentrations than currently acceptable, resulting in a more brittle material than modern steel. It was thought that after she had struck the iceberg, the added pressure of the water rushing in through one of the adjacent bulkheads proved too much for this damaged bulkhead, causing its collapse and accelerating the sinking.

The second issue was the excess steam, and therefore speed, generated by the fire. The only way to put out a coal fire was to shovel out the coal in the bunker until the burning coals could be found. With Titanic's coal bunkers each capable of holding 325 tons of it, this proved no small task, especially given it had to be done by hand. Unfortunately, the only place this coal could be shoveled to was into the boilers, which in turn created more steam, generating speed for the ship. It was a perfect storm—Titanic, despite multiple ice warnings, was exponentially increasing her speed right into a large ice field.

3

Mr. Andrews's suite was cabin A-36. I considered taking the lift, but decided against it in favor of admiring more of the ship. I realize I've potentially (okay, most assuredly) overstated it, but it really was a breathtaking piece of engineering. A-36 was just off of the aft staircase, on the port side of the ship. As I stood in front of the door, I began to doubt myself and this mission. *Could I really do this?* I thought. *What if I fail?* I did what I could to push those thoughts from my mind and knocked on the door.

A moment later the door opened and I was greeted by Mr. Andrews, holding a cup of (I assumed) tea. "Ah, Mr. Lawson. Good morning to you, sir. Please, come in."

"Good morning, Mr. Andrews," I said, stepping into the stunning first class suite. It was roughly double the size of my cabin, not that I was complaining, and the luxurious feel of it made mine seem downright pitiful.

"Can I offer you some tea? England's finest."

"Yes, that would be great. Just black, please."

He poured me a cup in the finest china and handed it to me, the friendly smile once again present. "The only way to have it, if you ask me."

I took a seat at the table with Andrews and took a sip of

the tea. It really was quite good. Once again I found myself a bit in awe. *I'm sitting in Thomas Andrews's cabin on the Titanic, and we're having tea.* Never in a hundred lifetimes would I have thought this moment could happen. Life is unpredictable like that.

"Thank you for the tea, it's wonderful."

"Of course," he said. "So, how are things? Accommodations okay?"

"All is well," I said, taking another sip of tea. "The accommodations onboard have been really quite extraordinary. I'm down in C-73."

His expression turned to one of almost embarrassment, or maybe disappointment—I wasn't quite sure. He shook his head. "C Deck? No, no, that just won't do."

"Sir?"

"I won't have a master engineer appointed by Her Majesty, onboard a ship I built, staying in any cabin but the best. Let me get you a suite here on A Deck. We have available cabins."

"That's not necessary, really. The cabin is great. But, there is something I wanted to ask of you, if it isn't too much trouble."

He sat his tea down and gave me his full attention. "Rest assured, Mr. Lawson, if it's in my power to do so, you shall have it. What can I do for you?"

I hesitated, wondering how he would respond. After all, what I did for Hanna was very much not the norm, but I've told you that already. I took another sip of my tea while organizing my thoughts.

"There's this woman onboard," I began. "I came upon her on my way to dinner last night. She's apparently a stowaway, just down on her luck, and two officers were going to take her down below and keep her there until New York." I couldn't help but cringe as the words came out of my mouth, knowing the ship would never make it there.

Andrews nodded, his attentiveness never faltering. So much so, in fact, it was becoming a distraction. I managed to focus my attention and continue with my reason for being there.

"I couldn't help but feel bad for her, so I offered to take custody of her for the duration of our trip."

"That was quite generous of you, Mr. Lawson. Most unusual, but indeed quite generous. Please, carry on."

Why did I come here? I'm going to make things very uncomfortable.

"Uh, well… I was hoping you'd be able to provide her with a cabin of her own as well as some proper attire." I immediately regretted asking. I shook my head. "I"m sorry, sir. I shouldn't have even come. I just thought it—"

He put up a hand. "Please, Mr. Lawson, you need not apologize. After all, you're a master engineer of Her Majesty!" He took a sip of his tea before standing up and slipping on his jacket. "As I said before, if it's in my power to do so, you shall have it… and if I may say, this is very much within my power. I will make sure your lady friend has whatever she desires in terms of accommodations while onboard."

I felt a wave of relief pass over my whole body. "Are you certain it isn't too much trouble?"

He laughed briefly, followed by a genuine smile. "A cabin and some clothes for the lady? Come now, Mr. Lawson, I hardly think that amounts to any level of trouble… particularly with all things considered." He took out his watch and checked the time. "You'll have to excuse me now, though, I have a meeting with Mr. Ismay in five minutes. Rest assured

I'll have my steward get your lady friend a cabin and a wardrobe of clothes."

I smiled, although I still couldn't quite believe it. "Thank you very much, Mr. Andrews. It means a lot, really." I stood up and extended my hand. "I will try not to interrupt your trip any further."

He laughed again and shook my hand. "You know, Mr. Lawson, you're an interesting fellow, I must say. For someone with such a high standing, you act as though you deserve nothing. Hold your head high, sir!"

We left his cabin together, and as he headed towards the Boat Deck, I went to tell Hanna the good news. Andrews assured me the cabin would be ready within a half hour. I knew none of this was relevant at all to my mission, desperately so in fact, but I just couldn't help myself. I was hoping I wouldn't come to regret it.

4

"You really mean it?" asked Hanna.

I nodded, having just finished telling her about my conversation with Mr. Andrews. "You will have your own cabin and wardrobe, ideally close to mine."

She hugged me, tighter this time, and I heard her sniffle. She let go a moment later and her eyes stared intently into mine.

"Such an enigma," she said. "I would have thought for sure you'd be trying to get me in bed with this kind of treatment."

I was about to respond when a knock at the door interrupted—it was my steward.

"Good morning, Mr. Lawson." He looked past me at

Hanna. "Miss." He bowed slightly. I turned back briefly and saw her blushing.

"Good morning, Smethells. How are things?"

"Very good, sir. I bring word from Mr. Andrews regarding a cabin and wardrobe for the lady." He presented me with a metal tray, on it a key with a label reading *C-71. Right next to mine*, I thought, a smile forming on my face. "The wardrobe in her cabin has been filled with a selection of outfits."

"Appreciate it, Smethells. Thank you."

He bowed briefly and turned to leave. "Please let me know if you or the lady need anything." And then he was gone.

I turned back to Hanna. "Come on, let's go get you settled." She followed me out into the hall and just to the right we stopped in front of C-71. I handed her the key. "Your key, m'lady." She was hesitant but took it anyway. She unlocked the door and stepped inside, myself following behind her. I heard her gasp.

"Oh, Andrew," she said, turning around and around trying to take in the entire room. "It's beautiful!" Her eyes found the wardrobe in the back corner, and she opened it, revealing over a dozen dresses. She looked through the first couple before closing it and turning to me, tears streaming down her face.

"What's wrong?" I asked.

She shook her head. "I—I can't accept this." She tried handing me the key back. "You've already done way too much for me, Andrew."

I pushed her hand back. "That's not true." I pulled her close to me, doing my best to comfort her. "Just because society feels you aren't of a certain class doesn't mean that's how you should be treated."

She managed to compose herself, at least a little. "I don't

know, Andrew. Something about your treatment of me is still suspicious. I'm used to fending for myself, even when I was married I was more or less on my own. So, this sort of kindness forces me to wonder why you're doing it. Does that make sense?"

I nodded. "It does, but I'm just trying to be a good person."

She contemplated this a moment before responding. "Thank you, Andrew. I'll never be able to repay you, of course. Not even close."

I smiled once more. "I wouldn't dream of asking you to." I looked at my watch, which said it was nearly nine. "I'm going to let you get settled here. I have some work I need to attend to. Will you be okay?"

"I think so," she said, looking around the room. "I'm free to roam the ship?"

I nodded, but in my head I was saddened by her question. Not that she asked, but that she felt the need to. *Imagine being afraid to leave your room.*

"You're a first class passenger now, Hanna. You can come and go as you please, save for the restricted crew areas of the ship."

A few moments and hugs from Hanna later, I was back in the hall and alone with my thoughts. They weren't particularly happy thoughts, either. *What if I'm messing up history by helping her? She was meant to be a stowaway, meant to be down below in custody.* I ultimately put it out of my mind. After all, the ship was meant to sink regardless, so whether or not I helped her out was irrelevant. I turned my attention, finally, to the real reason I was there.

5

Since I more or less had unrestricted access to the ship, I decided to visit the very bowels of it—the boiler rooms. One of the more controversial facts, which I've already told you a bit about, was the coal fire that had been burning uncontrollably since (supposedly) Titanic was in Belfast. Over the years I'd read countless articles, books, interviews, and anything else I could get my hands on regarding the ship's history. It was nearly impossible to find more than one or two sources that agreed on the severity of (or even the existence of) the fire. I needed to see for myself.

After leaving Hanna in her cabin, I took the aft staircase down to F Deck and after several failed attempts managed to pull from my memory of how to get down to the Tank Top, the lowest deck of the ship. I was quite thankful for my extensive knowledge of Titanic's layout—it made navigating her significantly easier. Even so, I found myself having to think back to the many hours of studying blueprints to remember how to get to certain places. This also played well into my portrayal of a master engineer.

Because the fire (if it really existed) occurred in a coal bunker between the fifth and sixth boiler rooms, I skipped over the first five and found my way into the sixth. Upon entering, I was immediately greeted with a wave of the hottest air I'd ever felt. I'd of course read plenty about the terrible conditions these brave men worked in, but experiencing it first-hand was another thing entirely. Just imagine the hottest sauna you've ever been in but a thousand times worse. It took my breath away. And it wasn't just the heat—the toxic fumes generated from the hundreds of tons of burning coal made it near impossible to breathe.

The Titanic had twenty-nine boilers, twenty four of which were double-ended, and five were single-ended. Each of these boilers was 15.7 feet in diameter, twenty feet long, and weighed 101 tons. These massive iron giants were fed around the clock by 179 firemen, consuming an enormous 600 tons of coal each day. It was because of the backbreaking work these men did that allowed enough steam to be generated to power not only the ship's propellers, but all of her luxurious accommodations. Unfortunately, these workers would never receive the praise (or compensation) they deserved.

Once I managed to compose myself, and my body had acclimated to the swamp-like environment, I cautiously began to look around. The room was filled with the sound of coal being shoveled into boilers by stokers, trimmers pushing wheelbarrows full of coal, and the leading fireman shelling out orders. Luckily for me, the leading fireman on duty now was just the person I had hoped to find—Mr. Frederick William Barrett.

Frederick Barrett was born in Lancashire, England in 1883. Funny enough, there was another fireman onboard Titanic with the exact same name. Unfortunately, only the one currently on duty would survive the sinking, making it off the ship in lifeboat #13. I knew Mr. Barrett had been one of the men directly involved in the coal bunker fire, so it was imperative that I spoke to him.

"Mr. Barrett?"

The man turned suddenly, and at first he scowled. "What's this? A passenger, down here? How'd you even—" It was then I saw his eyes shift to my badge. "Oh, my apologies, sir. I didn't notice right away." He stood at attention and turned to the men behind him.

"Master engineer present!" he shouted. Immediately, all the stokers and trimmers in the area stopped what they were doing and stood at attention. *This is weird.*

I put up my hand and shook my head. "At ease, men. I appreciate it, but it's not necessary, really."

They all returned to their duties as Fred turned back to face me.

"I'm Lead Fireman Barrett, that's right. Something I can do for you, sir?"

Barrett was a lanky man. His black hair, high and tight on the sides with a bit of length on top, at the moment was covered with soot and sweat. He had on suspenders over a plain white (also covered in coal soot) t-shirt.

"My name is Andrew Lawson. Do you have a moment to talk?"

He hesitated, my guess is because of the coal fire and not knowing whether to disclose it to me. All of the crew had been told to *keep their mouths shut* regarding anything about said fire. If asked, they were to say everything was going according to plan—nothing at all to worry about. I had a feeling about Barrett though. I figured he would talk.

"We're a bit swamped down here, Mr. Lawson. If you—"

"With the coal fire, right?" I asked, interrupting him. "Burning since Belfast, and you've just now discovered how severe it is."

His face told me what I needed to know. His eyes grew to twice their normal size, and if it hadn't been as hot as it was, I imagine sweat would have started at that point.

He pointed to a ladder just behind me. "I can spare two minutes. Let's chat up top where it's a bit quieter."

I scaled the ladder right after Mr. Barrett, my mind racing about what would be said. *Do I tell him anything? Everything?* I decided to let him speak first, which didn't turn out to be an issue.

"I suppose since you're a master engineer, I shouldn't be

surprised you know already, but how could you possibly know about the severity? My men and I only just got a handle on that no more than two hours ago."

If you hadn't noticed already, I found myself often saying too much for my own good on this trip. I knew it was important for me to watch what I said to avoid any unwanted attention, but more often than not it proved quite difficult to do. Thankfully, as was the case in many of the instances, I was able to talk around it.

I shook my head. "You wouldn't believe me if I told you, Mr. Barrett. But, having you confirm that it is as serious as expected helps me a great deal." So, after years of reading countless articles on the topic, I finally had proof that there was indeed a coal fire burning out of control on Titanic's maiden voyage. I needed to see it for myself.

A shout from below caught us both off guard.

"Mr. Barrett!" shouted one of the stokers. "The fire is rolling hotter, sir. You'd better get down here!"

"Ah hell," said Barrett. "Sounds like trouble. Look, Mr. Lawson, I don't know exactly what you're after down here, but if you want to hear it straight, this smoldering colossal should have never left her birth in Belfast. And that's just the truth, sir."

He nodded to me and disappeared down the ladder in an instant, leaving me bewildered by his departing statements. *It must be bad down there,* I thought. A moment later I climbed back down the ladder and made my way to the starboard side coal bunker. A moment later I was watching several stokers desperately emptying coal from the smoldering bunker. *This is happening. There really was an out of control coal fire, and I'm watching it happen.*

After staring at the bunker for another moment or two I

figured I had seen enough. Even if I told Fred the truth about Titanic's fate, I don't think there'd be anything he could do about it. I sighed and brushed the soot off my suit as I stopped to take a break on F deck. I still didn't know how I was going to stop the ship from sinking, but the solution wasn't in the boiler rooms. I was back to square one.

6

On my way back to my cabin I ran into Mr. Andrews, who was talking on A Deck with a well-dressed man of about fifty. His slicked black hair and handlebar mustache were unmistakable. This man was none other than Joseph Bruce Ismay, the chairman of The White Star Line. They both turned to me as I came up the grand staircase from B Deck.

"Ahh, Mr. Lawson," said Mr. Andrews. "Spare a moment?"

I nodded and came over to the men. "Hello, Mr. Andrews." I turned to Bruce. Hello, Mr. Ismay."

His expression remained mostly flat with a glimpse of a smirk as he nodded at me. "A master engineer onboard, eh? Hopefully everything is to your liking, Mr. Lawson."

"Oh yes, very much so," I said.

While I might be able to convince Mr. Andrews about the sinking, I knew better than to mention anything of the sort to Ismay. Every article I've read specifically calls out that he was one of the biggest supporters of the Titanic being unsinkable.

Born in Liverpool, England in 1862, Bruce Ismay would survive the sinking by escaping on collapsible lifeboat C. However, his luck would quickly run out, and for the rest of his life he was branded a coward and largely shunned by the public.

"Bruce and I were just talking about getting a late breakfast. Care to join us? I think Captain Smith will be there, too. I know he's been eager to meet you."

I felt my heart race at the mention of Smith. *Breakfast with the captain of Titanic? Pinch me, I must be dreaming.* Despite my giddiness, I managed to maintain my outward composure and responded.

"That would be great," I said.

"Splendid," said Andrews. "Let's go straight away."

CHAPTER VI

1

It was half past nine that morning when I sat down at the large round table in the dining saloon on D Deck. At the table was Thomas Andrews, Second Officer Lightoller, Captain Smith, First Officer Murdoch, Bruce Ismay, and myself. To say I was nervous would be a colossal understatement—even if the idea of feeling that way was silly when I really thought about it. While these men (with the exception of Thomas) didn't know me at all, save for my fictitious title, I knew every detail about their lives—both on and off the Titanic. Nevertheless, I couldn't help but feel the anxiety rising in my throat anytime I was mentioned.

"So, Mr. Lawson," said Smith. "I suspect you're working on a report of Titanic's maiden voyage, yes?"

Ahhh, was what my brain was doing at that moment. *The Captain of Titanic is addressing me.* I somehow managed a coherent response.

"I am, but not for any official business, I can assure you."

"Is that right?" he asked, taking a drink of his coffee.

"I'm simply enjoying the lavish accommodations The White Star has made available, and making some journal entries here and there about my experiences onboard."

Smith nodded. "Very good. If there's anything you need, make sure you reach out to one of my officers or Mr. Andrews or Ismay. They'll take care of you."

"Yes, sir. Mr. Andrews has already been most helpful."

He smiled, "Good, good." He took another bite of food. "Oh," he began again, "when you have a moment, you must come see the bridge. Perhaps after our meal this morning."

"That would be great," I said. After all, what else do you say when the Captain of (at the time) the largest and most luxurious ship in the world asks you to come visit its bridge.

The rest of the meal was filled with discussions about various things related to the ship and her trip across the Atlantic. Falling in line with what most articles said about him, Ismay was most concerned with the speed at which Titanic would reach New York. He was speaking in a hushed manner with Smith (albeit still very much audible to the rest of the table) about increasing her speed to get into port on the evening of Tuesday the 16th as opposed to the planned 17th.

Despite maintaining my own conversation with Thomas, my mind was much more focused on theirs. Knowing what I did made Ismay's attitude toward speed much more infuriating. The fact that Titanic continued to increase her speed throughout the journey, undeterred by the multiple ice warnings that they had received, was one of the prevailing theories around why they didn't see the iceberg in time—and why they weren't able to stop or maneuver around it. Even though I was frustrated, and even once caught myself clenching my fists, I didn't say anything—I couldn't. As much as I wanted to just blurt out everything I knew about what was going to happen, master engineer aside, I'd likely be taken down below by the master at arms, ruining my mission altogether.

2

After breakfast I followed Captain Smith and Officer Lightoller up to the bridge. As we were walking, I came to the conclusion I would tell Hanna the truth about why I was here. I felt like I had to tell someone—why not her?

"Welcome to the bridge, Mr. Lawson," said Smith. "This is Mr. Hichens." The man at the helm gave a quick wave towards me, which I returned.

Fun fact, the Titanic actually had four wheels in total. The main wheel, which was housed inside the fittingly named wheelhouse, was connected to the master control of the telemotor. Directly forward of the wheelhouse was a second wheel, this one being connected directly to the master wheel by a shaft and gear. This caused one wheel to turn when the other was turned. The third wheel, which is much less known about is located aft on the Docking Bridge, just above the Poop Deck (no jokes now). As the name would imply, this wheel was only used when docking at port. Finally, the fourth wheel, known as a "trick" wheel, was connected to the vertical shaft of the Docking Bridge wheel. This one was reserved for engineers below when they were working on one or both of the engines and needed to adjust the steering.

Edward John Smith, born January 27th, 1850 in Stoke, England, was the most senior officer of the White Star Line. He had served as the commanding officer for many of the company's liners, primarily on their maiden voyages. Smith was highly regarded among his colleagues but also the passengers. So much so, in fact, that the richest of the rich would schedule their trips across the Atlantic to align with when he would be commanding the ship.

Captain Smith led me to his sitting room, which was just behind the Wheel House on the starboard side. We discussed my time on board, of course, and he made sure I knew to let him or one of his officers know if there was anything I needed. The experience was quite surreal, and despite knowing what I did about his (potential) fate, I managed to keep myself composed.

I talked with Captain Smith for a few more minutes before taking my leave. He said he was late for something anyway, and invited me to dinner tomorrow evening. *Well, I'm fitting in nicely at least,* I thought. Unfortunately, I hadn't made any headway at all with my mission. *I need to stop getting distracted.* I made my way back down to C Deck and into my cabin. I wanted time to myself before going to visit Hanna again. I needed to think.

3

I paced around my room, determined not to leave until I had at least the makings of a plan. Okay, time to think this through. It was the morning of April 11th—three days and some change until Titanic would meet her doom. The obvious solution of simply telling Captain Smith (or any of the officers) was out of the question. I couldn't risk being detained. Besides, the likelihood of them believing a word I said was low. I could potentially tell Mr. Andrews, being the more understanding one of them all, but it was still risky. I needed alternatives.

What about the wireless? I knew morse code, at least a

little. If I could get into the wireless room, maybe I could send a message to a nearby ship. I shook my head. What good would that do? What would I say?

"Hey, uh... this is the Titanic. Say, we're going to hit an iceberg in three days... could you make sure to be nearby?"

Yeah, that would get loads of responses.

I wish James was here—he would know what to do.

I reached back into the far corners of my memory, desperate for any piece of history I had on the ship that could be helpful. An idea came to me then—the ice warnings. While it was well-documented that for the most part, Titanic ignored the ice warnings she received, Captain Smith had made a slight course correction due to one of the reports from the RMS Baltic. Because of this, my thoughts went to the last ice warning received on the night of April 14th.

This last ice warning, received at 9:40 p.m. from the SS Missaba, reported the sighting of numerous large icebergs directly in the path of the Titanic. Unfortunately, the message hadn't contained an MSG prefix, which in morse code meant the message was for the master of the ship, i.e. Captain Smith. Because of this, Smith nor any of the officers ever received that fifth and most vital of the ice warnings—as far as anyone knows, of course. As the saying goes, dead men tell no tales.

I thought this idea over in my head. If I could time it right and get myself into the wireless room around the time this last warning was received, perhaps I could swipe it and ensure Smith sees it. Of course, there was a glaring issue with this idea as well. If I went this route, that would mean I'd be waiting until the very last minute to act. The last ice warning came just two hours before the collision. If this plan failed, my mission was over. I shook my head again and kicked one of the chairs in frustration.

Maybe the ship wasn't saveable. I put the thought out of my mind as soon as it surfaced. No, I was here to save the Titanic, and I wasn't about to give up on her—not yet at least. There had to be something I was missing, there had to be. Ugh, why did men in this era have to be so arrogant and reluctant to have their beliefs challenged. I realized a short time after thinking this that men of my time weren't all that different. Some things never change, as they say. A knock at the door brought me out of the trenches of my thoughts.

As I opened the door, Hanna greeted me. She was wearing one of the dresses from the wardrobe, the subtle lavender of it reminded me of Spring. I realized she must have heard my relentless pacing and kicking of chairs.

"Ah, hello Hanna," I said, scratching at the back of my head. "Sorry if I disturbed you. Won't you come in?"

She smiled and stepped inside. "You didn't disturb me," she said, taking a seat at the small circular table. "I thought I heard your door a bit ago and wanted to see how things were going with your business."

My business, right. At times it was easy to forget about my master engineer cover. "It's going well. I'm not here on any official business from Her Majesty. No, this trip is just for my enjoyment."

She nodded. "I see. Look, Mr. Lawson—"

"Please, call me Andrew."

"Right, sorry. Anyway, Andrew, I wanted to thank you once again for what you did. I still don't know why, and maybe I never will, but just know I am very grateful."

As I sat across from her at the table, I met her eyes and saw the sincerity in them. The dress looked wonderful on her, fitting surprisingly well for being from another passenger. Her fiery red hair, which had been recently washed, reached just past her shoulders and complimented her fair complexion. *She was beautiful,* I thought. *But I can't. I can't let my feelings come into this, it's too risky, not to mention utterly distracting.*

"You're most welcome," I said. "But again, I was just doing what was right. By the way, you look lovely in that dress."

Her smile brightened, the most I'd seen so far. I saw a bit of redness form on her cheeks as well.

"Thank you, Mr—I mean, Andrew." She hesitated for a moment, and I saw her fidgeting with her hands. "Would you care to join me on a walk around the Boat Deck? I'm eager to see the view, and your company would make it all the better. If you don't mind, of course."

I looked at my watch, aghast at the fact it was already a quarter after twelve. I'd been pacing in my room for over an hour, making it even more unfortunate that I still didn't have a plan. The thought of taking a walk up on the Boat Deck with Hanna sounded lovely, however, so I made an exception to my earlier rule of not leaving until I had made a plan.

"I'd be happy to," I said, putting away my watch and grabbing my suit jacket. "Perhaps afterwards we can have lunch in the Cafe Parisian? I hear their food is excellent." I know, I know… further delaying the development of a plan—I couldn't help it.

"That would be very nice," she said, standing up from her chair. "Shall we?"

I extended my arm, just as I had last night when we first met, and after she put her arm in mine we left my cabin for the Boat Deck.

4

Titanic's Boat Deck was the topmost of the ship's ten decks, and as the name would imply, it was where the lifeboats were stored. It was constructed of fresh teak wood and divided into four segregated promenades; the Officer's Promenade, First Class area, Engineers, and Second Class areas. Sixteen lifeboats (four collapsible boats were stored on top of the Officers's quarters) lined either side of the Boat Deck, odd numbered on the starboard side and even on the port side. Even though there was more than sufficient room remaining to accommodate additional lifeboats, only these precious sixteen were approved—only enough for about half of the passengers onboard. And this was assuming they'd be filled to capacity (65), which they were not.

I do feel the need to point out a glaring misconception about Titanic and the lifeboat situation. Were there grossly too few onboard compared to her passenger count? Absolutely. No question there. That being said, the idea that if there had been forty-eight lifeboats approved, as Mr. Andrews requested, there was still no guarantee that all of the passengers and crew would have survived. In fact, on that cold morning of April 15th, the officers weren't even able to prepare and launch the twenty boats that were onboard. It's ultimately a much more complicated answer than is generally known by the public, and one I won't continue to dwell on here.

As Hanna and I exited out the Grand Staircase door onto the Boat Deck, we were immediately greeted by the chilly breeze coming off the ocean. We walked aft along the starboard side of the ship. Going towards the bow would have meant passing through the Officer's Promenade, and while I would be allowed, I didn't want to cause any issues with getting Hanna approval to do so.

"Are you liking your cabin?" I asked.

"Oh yes, it's beautiful. And these dresses, they're stunning!"

I smiled. "I'm glad you like them."

We continued on in silence for a moment or two, enjoying the beautiful views Titanic had to offer. The weather was clear, lending to us being able to see a great distance across the Atlantic.

"So," said Hanna, breaking the silence, "what exactly does a 'master engineer' do?"

A fair question, I thought. How to answer? I didn't know what a master engineer did any more than she did. In fact, I'm pretty certain there was no such thing. Nevertheless, I was good at winging my way through situations, so I did my best to make up something.

"It's quite boring, really. My main duty is to accompany ships, often on their maiden voyages, and take note of anything I encounter that requires additional investigation. Once I reach the ship's destination I'll compile my notes and send a report to the appropriate people."

She faked a yawn, smiling. "My, that does sound rather dull. Do you enjoy it?"

"I do. I've always found maritime history fascinating, and having the opportunity to see as many ships as this job allows me to is a dream come true."

"Good. I think it's important to enjoy what you do."

As we rounded the aft-most part of the Boat Deck and proceeded onto the port side, Hanna stopped, looking up towards the sky.

"Okay, Mr. Master Engineer, I have a question for you."

"Sure." No reason not to be confident. The odds of her asking me a question about the ship I didn't know were remote.

"I've been noticing that this fourth funnel seems to be releasing much less fumes than the other three… almost none, actually. Is something wrong with it?"

An easy one, I thought.

"Nope, nothing wrong with it at all. The fourth funnel exists primarily to even out the total number. Titanic only has three engines, but that doesn't mean the fourth serves no purpose. It's also used to ventilate the kitchen as well as the smoking room."

"Huh, interesting," she said, looking up once more at the funnel before facing me again. "Tell me more about the ship, master engineer." She chuckled at herself. It made me smile seeing her relax a bit and show her true self.

We had reached the port side entrance to the grand staircase, opposite where we started. I felt myself taking a liking to Hanna—for better or worse.

"How about I talk to you about the Titanic over lunch?" I motioned towards the staircase door, opening it for her. "The Café Parisien is two decks down on B Deck."

She stepped through as I followed. "Do you know where every room is onboard?"

I lead the way, taking the staircase down to B Deck and heading aft. "For the most part," I replied. "I suppose there might be a room or two I'd have to think on, but I could tell you the location of a good majority of this ship's rooms and how to get there from anywhere else onboard."

She whistled and playfully hit me on the shoulder. "That's pretty impressive. I might have to test you on that."

5

A few moments later we sat down in the cafe at a table

towards the back. There were a few other passengers among us, but for the most part we had the place to ourselves. It was after one that afternoon, so we had missed the rush of lunchtime. We kept it simple, both of us having a sandwich and coffee, two of the more common items served in the cafe.

"This is a lovely part of the ship," said Hanna, taking in the white lattice and greenery, both of which were plentiful in the cafe. "Not very busy, either."

"I agree, it's a quaint place to get a quick meal. So, you wanted to know more about Titanic?"

She took a large bite of her sandwich, hers was turkey I think, and sipped her coffee before responding. "How long did it take to build?"

"They started construction on March 31st, 1909 and was completed exactly three years later. She had sea trials two days later, followed by departing to Southampton in preparation for her maiden voyage."

As I took a quick sip of coffee, I noticed her eyes were locked onto mine, apparently taking in every word I said.

"You sure know a great deal about this ship."

I lifted my badge that was around my neck, grinning. "It's kind of my job to know."

"I suppose that's true." She sipped her coffee and looked out one of the port holes, the endless blue of the Atlantic filling her view.

As she turned back to me and took another bite of her sandwich, the mentioning of my "job" brought my mind racing back to the reason I was here. *I have to tell her,* I thought. *Even if she doesn't believe me, at least I told someone.*

"Can I ask you a question?" I asked, finishing my coffee and setting the cup off to the side of the table.

She nodded with a smile. "It's only fair."

"Do you ever think about the future?" Okay, I'll admit the question was a little on the nose, but I wanted to see what her mindset was like before dumping my true identity on her.

"The future?" After a moment of contemplating she sighed and shook her head. "No, not really. I used to look forward to it, back when I was married and happy. But now I just do what I can to get through each day. Although, I must admit, the past two days have been most wonderful thanks to you."

This wasn't quite the answer I was expecting, but it wasn't at all surprising either.

"Fair enough," I said.

We spent another forty-five minutes or so at the cafe, which mainly consisted of Hanna asking me random questions about the ship. How many rooms were there, how fast could she go, and a number of others—all of which I was happy to answer. I don't think there was any particular reason she was wanting to know such details about the ship—I think she just enjoyed my company, and this was a topic she knew I was interested in. It was half past three when I decided it was time to tell her everything. Worst case, she didn't believe me and I'd just figure out what to do on my own.

6

We made our way down to C Deck and back into my cabin. As I closed the door and turned to face Hanna, she was right behind me, a smile on her face. A moment later she was kissing me, her body firmly pressed against mine. I felt butterflies in my stomach at the softness of her lips on mine. *No, no,* I thought. *This can't happen.* I gently pushed her back, not wanting her to think I didn't like her or anything—I really did like her.

Her face told me I failed at this. "I don't understand, don't you like me?"

A deep sigh escaped my lips before I could hold it back. "It's not that, Hanna."

"Then what?"

I motioned towards the chairs at the table. "Could we sit? It's complicated."

Begrudgingly, she followed me over to the chairs and we sat down. I felt my heart beating more and more quickly in my chest as I tried to figure out how on earth to explain everything to Hanna.

"So, what's going on? I thought things were going well between us." I saw the pain on her face, not crying yet but close. *This is going to be hard.* "Please, Andrew, just tell me."

"I'm not from here." It just came out—I didn't even think about it.

"What do you mean 'here'? We're in the middle of the Atlantic, of course you're not from here."

Another sigh escaped my lips. "I mean, I'm not from this time… from 1912." I paused, my heartbeat rising to a dangerous level, and finally spoke the words I wasn't sure I'd ever be able to say. "I'm from the future."

A blank expression came over her face with her mouth hanging open. She sat in silence at first, trying to comprehend what I had just said—I couldn't blame her.

"The future? I don't understand. Is this some kind of joke? Are you just stringing me on or something?"

I shook my head. "No, it's the truth. Where I'm from, in the future, we have the technology to travel through time."

She stared blankly at me, and for a moment silence fell between us. She finally managed to speak.

"H—how far in the future?"

I sighed. "107 years."

She put a hand over her mouth and gasped. "107 years?" I saw her do some quick math in her head. "So, you're from the year 2019?" I nodded. "But, how? I don't understand."

How—I was not in much of a position to explain time travel to anyone, especially not to someone from a time when cell phones weren't yet a thing. This was another time when I wished James had come with me, but I had to say something —anything.

"It's complicated, and I don't honestly understand it very well myself. A person much smarter than myself sent me here."

"Okay, let's say I believe you, which is still very much up for debate. Why 1912? Why the Titanic? It's not going to sink or something, right?"

She let out a light chuckle and tried to lighten up the mood. As my expression remained serious after her comment, the already meager smile was replaced by horror as she realized the truth.

"Oh, oh god. That's it, isn't it? The Titanic is going to sink."

I nodded. "Yes." I wanted to say more, but being caught up in the moment was rendering my brain useless.

Hanna stood up and began pacing around my cabin. She stopped after a moment and turned back to face me.

"How is it going to sink? Do you know? Of course you do."

It took me a second, but I managed to force my brain back into the conversation at hand, which I was thankful for.

Hanna would have a number of questions, of that I was certain.

"An iceberg… one of the largest ever recorded."

She shook her head. "But isn't the Titanic supposed to be unsinkable? That's what everyone says. Maybe it gets damaged or something, but surely it won't sink, right?"

"That's an unfortunate misnomer, I'm afraid. No ship is unsinkable, Hanna. Even in my time we have ships that sink. Not as often, mind you, but they still do."

She sat back down across from me, the color in her face had all but vanished. "Please, if this is some kind of sick and twisted joke just to mess with a poor woman…"

It killed me to think she would consider that a possibility.

"It's not a joke, Hanna." I glanced at my watch—3:40 p.m. "In exactly three days and eight hours, the ship is going to strike the iceberg. Two hours and forty minutes later—" I motioned around the room with my arms. "All of this will be at the bottom of the Atlantic, along with over 1,500 lives."

Her hand went over her mouth again. "You know the exact time?"

"I know nearly everything there is to know about this ship."

She continued to stare at me, her eyes barely blinking. "This… this is unbelievable. You're sure about this? Titanic is the ship that sinks? What if you're wrong?" I could tell even she didn't believe her words.

"I'm not wrong, Hanna. The sinking of the Titanic will become the most well-known maritime disaster in history. Even in 2019, there's no disaster that comes close to gaining the notoriety that the early morning of April 15th will have."

"Wait a minute, 1,500 lives? Why so many? Are people not going to board lifeboats?"

"Oh no, they do. But, unfortunately, the ship has far too few lifeboats to accommodate all of her passengers. Less than half, in fact."

As I've already mentioned, the number of lifeboats wasn't solely responsible for those lost lives, but for the sake of my conversation with Hanna, I didn't bring up this point.

"What? Why?" She scoffed. "That's absurd!"

I nodded. "I agree. The truth is, there are a number of things that went wrong, as well as some things still to go wrong, that will ensure Titanic's fate. She was, as future author's will write, almost doomed before she set sail from Belfast."

She got up a second time and began to pace. I could hear her breathing increase, not that I could blame her, but I was worried she might spiral from the shock. I didn't break the news to her quite how I had wanted, but put yourself in my shoes. There's no great way to tell someone you're from 107 years in the future.

She stopped pacing again and turned to me, shaking her head. "No, no I don't believe you Mr. Lawson. I'm sorry, but something isn't right here." Before I could even get a word out, she was out the door, closing it quickly behind her. A moment later I heard the door to her cabin open and close.

I sighed and buried my face in my hands. *Well, that went about as well as I could have hoped.*

I spent a few more minutes at the table, replaying the conversation with Hanna in my head. While I had wanted to be more subtle in telling her the truth, I wasn't sure how I could have done so. I decided not to dwell on it too much, and instead I would take a walk around the ship. It was, after all, the largest in the world, so it offered plenty of room to stretch your legs.

7

Another fact not commonly known about the Titanic, was that a large portion of the original engineering crew (the ones who delivered her from Belfast) left the ship after their arrival at Southampton. It was believed by some that these men knew about the coal bunker fire and how serious it was. There was never any conclusive evidence of this being the reason behind the mass exodus, but after what I had seen on my second day onboard, I know it to be true. Those men were luckier than even they may have thought at the time.

While on the topic of crew changes, Captain Smith made a last-minute change of his own with the officers working under him. He gave Henry Wilde, who had served under him on Titanic's sister ship Olympic, the post of chief officer. This demoted the original appointee, William Murdoch, to first officer and Charles Lightoller to second officer. The original second officer, David Blair, was excluded from the maiden voyage altogether, the significance of which shall become immediately clear.

Frustrated, Mr. Blair made a hastened retreat from the Titanic, accidentally taking with him the key to the ship's binoculars. This was later determined to have played a vital role in the ship hitting the iceberg. If lookouts Fleet and Lee had had access to the binoculars, it's almost certain they would have spotted the berg significantly sooner—likely soon enough for the ship to navigate around it.

8

While I don't think I could ever get tired of walking around the Titanic, admiring the vast amount of lavish furnishings throughout the ship, it didn't manage to completely take my mind off of Hanna. I felt bad, and part of me wished I had never brought it up to her. But, it was too late for that, wasn't it? I just needed to do my best and focus on the task at hand.

I took another lap around the Boat Deck before venturing down to check out the Squash Racquet Court. While the actual court itself was way down on G Deck, the entrance was up on D Deck. The room measured 30' x 20', and actually had an instructor on staff, if you were interested in learning how to play. I believe his name was Mr. Wright, but either way, I was just there to see the court, not play.

A couple in their early sixties were in the middle of a game when I arrived. On F Deck there was a spectator's gallery, which gave an excellent view of the court. I sat and watched for nearly an hour before deciding to head back to C Deck. My mind kept telling me to knock on Hanna's door to see if she was okay, but I ultimately skipped it and went into my own cabin.

As I opened the door, I was surprised to see Hanna sitting at the table in the middle of the room. She looked up at me, and when I saw her eyes I could tell she'd been crying. I closed the door and hesitantly sat down in the opposite chair.

"Hi," I said.

She didn't return my greeting. "Look me in the eyes, Andrew, if that is your real name. Look me in the eyes and tell me what you told me earlier was the truth."

I held her gaze, her eyes still had the kindness I first saw, but there was now fear, perhaps uncertainty and frustration as well.

"Hanna, what I said was the truth. My name really is

Andrew Lawson, and I'm from the year 2019. I'm here to stop the sinking of the Titanic."

She held my stare for a few more seconds before letting out a heavy sigh and rubbing her eyes. She got up and walked over to my side of the table and gave me an awkward hug while I was still sitting.

"Okay," she said. "I believe you. I don't understand it at all, but I believe you."

I was relieved. At the very least I had one person on this ship who I could be completely honest with.

"So, what's your plan for saving the ship?"

It was my turn to sigh. "I don't have one… not a solid one anyway."

"You don't have a plan? I thought that's why you came here in the first place."

I didn't need the reminder, but I deserved to hear it. The truth was, I had all but wasted my first two days onboard. Although, I did meet Hanna, so not a total waste, but none of it would matter if I didn't figure out a way to stop it from sinking.

"Unfortunately, it's not that simple. I can't just go up to Captain Smith and tell him what I told you. He'd say I was crazy and have the Master-at-Arms arrest me."

"But, you have very specific details about the accident. Surely if you tell him the exact time and location, along with the other things you just told me, he'd be inclined to believe you."

I shook my head. "You don't know these officers like I do. They're all blinded by their arrogance toward this ship and her abilities. Like you said, everyone sees her as unsinkable, and that opinion runs deep. And if that wasn't enough, Mr. Ismay is determined to set a new speed record in crossing the

Atlantic, so he's been urging Captain Smith to continue increasing Titanic's speed… despite multiple ice warnings."

She sighed and threw herself back down onto the chair. "There has to be something you can do, Andrew. Otherwise, all those people will lose their lives!" A sudden look of fear came over her. "Hey, wh—what happens to me? Am I a part of those 1,500?"

I shrugged. I didn't like how that action felt, given the circumstances, but it was all I could bring myself to do.

"I honestly don't know, Hanna. You were a stowaway, remember?"

She pursed her lips and then spoke. "Right." She ran her hands through her hair, thinking. "So, you don't have any ideas?"

"I have one for sure, but it's risky."

"Tell me."

Just then, a knock at the door.

CHAPTER VII

1

I remember feeling a heavy weight lifted from my shoulders after I told my story to Hanna. I was still stressed of course, knowing that the Titanic would sink in three days if I didn't do something about it, but at least someone onboard besides me knew the truth—knew the truth and believed it.

The knock on the door had been my steward, Smethells. He greeted us both happily and presented me with a card on a silver tray.

"A message for you, sir," he said. "From Mr. Andrews, I believe."

I took the card and read it.

Having dinner this evening with Captain Smith and other officers at 6:30. Hoping you and your lady friend can join us. Please pass along your decision to Smethells.

- Andrews

I smiled and turned to Hanna. "It's an invitation for dinner tonight with the Captain and crew. Care to join me?"

"Dinner with the Captain? Oh, Andrew, I don't know. Are you sure you want me to come?"

"Of course I do. Just think of it this way… it'll give you another reason to wear more of the dresses in your new wardrobe."

This brought the smile back to her face. "I like that. Okay, yes I'll go!"

I turned back to Smethells, who was patiently waiting for my response. "Please let Mr. Andrews know the two of us happily accept his invitation."

He nodded. "Very good, sir. Will there be anything else?" I shook my head and he left.

"So," said Hanna, "how about this plan? Maybe I can help." I nodded as the two of us sat back down at the table.

"Thank you for believing me. I wasn't sure if you would, but it feels good to have someone else on my side here."

"I'll be honest, I still don't know for sure what to make of it. I mean, I want to believe you, and you have ample detail to back up your story… but you must understand how it sounds from my side."

I nodded. "Oh, absolutely. In fact, when the man who sent me here first tried to explain it to me, I also found it hard to believe. I'm sure I sound crazy to you, just like he did to me, but I swear it's the truth. If only there was a way I could—" *Hang on,* I thought. *Maybe there is a way.*

She waved her hand in front of me, seeing I was zoning out. "Andrew? You alright?"

"Hanna, how would you like to take a trip with me?"

"A trip? Whatever do you mean? To another part of the ship? What good would that do?"

I shook my head. "No, a trip to my time. To 2019. I could prove to you what I'm saying is true. And, maybe the three of us could figure out a plan together at the same time."

Her mouth gaped open as my words registered in her head. "To—to the future? You can just up and go like that?"

In all honesty, I wasn't certain I could. While James had been explaining the inner workings of time travel to me, my brain went into sleep mode. However, I do remember him giving me a secondary TR (transmitter/receiver) module to communicate back through the wormhole to the Anode Reactor. It was to only be used in emergencies, which I felt that this was close enough to one. I wanted Hanna to have zero doubts about the validity of the situation.

"I believe so, yes. The man who sent me back here gave me a device to help get me back in the event of something going wrong. I'm sure he'd understand if I take you back to convince you."

I could see she was contemplating everything I'd said, anxiety evident on her face. And who could blame her? A guy you've only known for two days suddenly tells you he's from 2019, and now he wants to take you back there. She'd have to be crazy herself to go along with me.

"Okay, I'll go with you. But Andrew, one question."

"Sure."

"If you can just travel on a whim through… through time… sorry, that's still hard for me to understand. Anyway, if you can just do that, why bother trying to save the Titanic while you're on it? Why not just go back to before the ship sets sail and find a way to stop it? I'd think that would make things much easier, no?"

She was right, of course. That would make this mission or plan, whatever you want to call it, a lot easier. Unfortunately, as you know from when James explained it to me, doing it that way wouldn't fix the ultimate problem. Good thinking on her part though. She's clever. I hope she can help me figure something out.

"It would make it significantly easier, yes. Unfortunately, I can't do that."

"Why not?"

I sighed. "It's complicated, I'm afraid. Really complicated. James, the guy who sent me here, could explain it much more succinctly than me, but I'll try." I took a second to remember what I'd been told. "Have you heard of the butterfly effect?"

She shook her head. "No, I don't think so. What does a butterfly have to do with time travel?"

I almost laughed, but I held it in. I didn't want to seem rude.

"The butterfly in this case is being used metaphorically. It's a phenomenon that basically says even minute changes, such as the fluttering of a butterfly's wings, can have dramatic effects on the future timeline. Are you with me?"

"I think so. Go on."

"So, in truth, the primary reason for me being back here is to save a man. His name is Cillian Hughes."

"A man? What's so important about this Cillian person?"

"That gets more complicated, and I'd really prefer to have James explain it. But, essentially, we need to have Cillian be unaware that we've intervened with the timeline, and have him complete his trip on Titanic as he originally did."

She put up her hands in a *stop* motion. "Hang on, what do you mean by 'as he originally did'? You lost me."

I shook my head. "I need James for this. Do you still want to go with me?"

She nodded. "I do. Is everything this complicated in the future?"

That question made me chuckle. "Not quite as complicated as time travel, no, but I would say overall things are more complicated than they are now."

"Well that's not very reassuring. Speaking of the future... Are you actually an engineer in your time? Or is that some ruse related to your mission?"

For a brief moment I had considered lying to her—telling her that I really was an engineer. But why? If this woman is willing to travel 107 years into the future with me, just on my word, I think she deserves the truth.

"No, I'm not an engineer. Coincidentally, I'm a history teacher with a fascination for the Titanic."

She smiles. "I guess that's why you're here." I nod. "Okay then, Andrew." She gets up and comes to me, wrapping her arms around me from behind and gives me a kiss on the cheek. "When do we leave?"

I turned back to face her, meeting those kind eyes of hers, and kissed her on the lips. She's surprised at first, but quickly kisses me back. The softness of her lips against mine causes my stomach to stir—it's a good feeling.

I stopped kissing her for a moment. "I—I think we should move to the bed first, and then figure out when to leave."

She nodded emphatically, starting to undo her dress. "I think that's a great idea, Mr. Lawson."

3

Okay, so I slept with a stowaway on the Titanic—sue me. There was just something about Hanna I couldn't quite put my finger on, as they say. Maybe it was her relentless determination to make a better life for herself, or maybe it was her beautiful caramel colored eyes flanked by her golden red hair. Or, a combination of those along with a number of other traits she had that I admired. Either way, she felt genuine to me, and I was grateful to have met her.

4

After satisfying both of our needs, I got up and found the TR device that James had sent with me. It was towards the bottom of one of my suitcases, tucked underneath my bespoke suits. I really need to make sure I thank him for those—they're fantastic. The device itself, however, was underwhelming in its appearance. It was made of metal, my guess is the same stuff James's Anode Reactor was made of, but I can't recall the name at the moment. To me it looked like an oversized drink coaster.

I sat the device on the table. "Here it is."

She started to reach for it but hesitated. "Is it safe?"

I nodded, picking it up and handing it to her. "It's heavier than it looks though."

She held onto it as if it were made of glass, or as if it were going to bite her. Not that I could blame her. Again, even I was taken aback by the technology this thing represented. And that metal—basically indestructible.

"How does it work?" She handed it back to me.

I got up, looking over the device. "Honestly? I don't know. When James gave it to me, he told me it would be apparent what to do with it."

She frowned. "Well, that's not very helpful."

I was about to agree when I saw an indentation on the underside of it. *It looks like a thumbprint.* I turned it over and put my right thumb in the indentation. A moment later there was a short beep followed by a computerized voice I recognized.

"Fingerprint confirmed. Hello, Mr. Lawson. Please place the TR device on a level surface."

Hanna's mouth nearly hit the table. "What... was that?"

I gently put the device onto the floor. "It's the AI that controls James's lab. Err, never mind. I'll explain it later. Or James will."

And then the voice spoke again.

"Please stand clear, the platform is about to expand."

I stepped away, pulling Hanna with me. The device suddenly expanded to a length of roughly three meters.

"Initializing time synchronization and locating AR source signal. AR signal acquired. Are you ready to commence wormhole transportation?"

We both stood for a moment in silence, unsure of whether to respond.

"Response not recognized. Are you ready to commence wormhole transportation?"

"Yes," I managed to say.

"Response confirmed. Please step onto the platform."

I felt Hanna squeeze my hand tightly at the voice's request. I stepped towards the device, pulling her gently behind me.

"It's okay," I said, making the worst attempt at comforting her. "Don't let go of my hand."

"Oh, I wasn't about to," she said, following me onto the device. "I don't know if I'm ready for this, Andrew. Does it hurt? What's going to happen? Will I be way older?"

I took my other hand and put it over hers.

"It doesn't hurt, but the first time you do it your stomach will feel like it's doing somersaults. And, I know this sounds crazy, but you'll get the feeling of an out-of-body experience. But there's no pain, I promise."

Her eyes widened as I felt her grip tighten again. "O—okay. What about my age?"

"You'll be the same as when you left here."

The voice interrupted her response. "Two life signs detected. All systems are online and ready. Do you wish to initiate?"

"Yes, initiate," I said, not giving either of us time to reconsider.

"Command confirmed. Initializing in 3… 2… 1."

5

I knew bringing Hanna back to James's lab wasn't a great idea. Bringing someone 107 years into the future was bound to cause all sorts of mental trauma. It might have been different if it had been 1812 to 1919, however, the technical advancements that have been accomplished between 1912 and 2019 are unparalleled. Me going back to the past wasn't all that jarring due to my extensive research on the time period surrounding the Titanic. But, I can't imagine the shock she must have felt in those first few moments after we arrived in the lab.

A white flash filled our vision, and then it was replaced with the same view of the lab I had just before leaving two days ago. Standing in front of us was James, flanked by the holographic project of Anansi on his right. He didn't seem surprised to see us, so he must have been alerted to the TR device activation. Hanna was in complete and utter shock—she couldn't even move from her spot on the platform.

"Brought a friend I see," said James, stepping towards us. "She's going to need a few minutes."

I sighed and nodded. "I know this device is for emergencies only, but I needed to prove to her my story was real. Things aren't going so great onboard."

He showed a look of understanding and turned his attention to Hanna.

"Miss, are you alright?"

I gently put my hand on her shoulder. She winced, but then turned to meet my eyes, which seemed to give her some calm.

"Are you okay?" I asked. "We made it. We're in 2019."

She looked to be about ready to say something when her eyes caught a glimpse of the holograph of Anansi. Her mouth dropped open, and I saw terror in her eyes.

"Wh—what in God's name is that?" She stumbled off the platform, nearly falling over before regaining her balance. "Andrew, what am I looking at?"

Where to begin?

"Uh, well… that's a bit hard to explain," I began. "Maybe we should start with introductions." I motioned towards James. "Hanna, this is James. He's the one who sent me back to the Titanic. James, this is Hanna. She was a stowaway that I saved while onboard."

"It's a pleasure," said James, extending his hand. "Welcome to my lab."

Hanna, who was still at her wits end, hesitantly took his hand and shook it. "Ni—nice to meet you, sir. What is all this? Am I really in the year 2019?"

James smiled and nodded. "This is my lab where I do my work. I'm a scientist. And yes, this is the year 2019. Andrew brought you back here with the help of my Anode Reactor, a time travel device I built."

Her mouth was gaping again as she turned her head in all directions, trying to take in everything. I understand exactly how overwhelming that moment was for her. Well, maybe not exactly, seeing as I was well-versed in the year 1912, but it still takes some getting used to. Despite it all, however, after the initial shock she took it fairly well.

She turned back to me. "So, everything you said back on the Titanic was true. The ship really does sink, and you came back to stop it."

"It's really going to sink, yes. Unless we come up with a plan, which I'm hoping the three of us can be more successful than I've been so far."

Hanna looked ashamed as her shoulders slumped. "I'm sorry I doubted you at all, Andrew. I do hope you'll forgive me."

"What? Please don't apologize, Hanna. From your perspective, you had every right to doubt me." I hugged her tightly, feeling her return the hug, and gave her a peck on the lips. "I'm just glad I was able to prove it to you."

"So," said James. "What's the trouble, Andrew? I'll of course help in any way I can."

I motioned towards the round table we had sat at together two days ago. "Let's have a seat. This could take awhile."

6

The three of us sat down along with Anansi's projection, who kept her distance from Hanna to avoid freaking her out even more. I was eager to find a solution, so I began talking almost as soon as we sat down.

"So, the biggest issue is the crew. I don't know how I didn't think of this before, probably because of how excited I was to actually see the Titanic in person." That got a laugh from James. Hanna was still not fully focused on the conversation, but that's to be expected. "Anyway, once I got onboard and was somewhat able to get my mind on the mission, I quickly realized there was no way I could convince any of the crew Titanic would sink. Her 'unsinkable' title would unfortunately stay with her until the bitter end."

James stood up and started to pace, his hands behind his back like a typical scientist. "That is a problem indeed," he said. "Even if you did decide to try convincing them, it's quite unlikely they'll believe a word you say."

"Exactly. There might be one I could tell, Thomas Andrews, but it's still not without great risk. If I were to be detained, it would mean the end of the mission."

Hanna raised her hand.

"Oh, that's not necessary here," I said. "We're just brainstorming. Speak your mind, Hanna."

She lowered her hand. "Well, I asked before we came here, but why can't James use his uh, the time thing, to send you back to before the Titanic takes her maiden voyage and stop it then?"

I turned to James. "I told her you could better explain this one."

"Of course," he said. "I'll do my best to explain, Hanna, but try to keep an open mind, okay?"

"I'm doing my best," she said. "This is… a lot."

He chuckled. "Yes, I would imagine so. Oh, and please forgive me for the shock caused by my AI." He motioned towards Anansi's hologram. "She's harmless, I promise."

"She? That's a human? What was it you said… an A.. I..?"

I wish I could have mentally prepared Hanna for the conversation she was about to have with James, but how could I? Thankfully, he didn't end up going too in-depth into the AI conversation, however, he still dropped a hefty amount of information on her. This was further troublesome due to her being from a time before land lines being commonplace. It just isn't something you can prepare someone for. But, if James could explain time travel to a history teacher, maybe he could do the same for a stowaway from 1912.

James smiled. "Not quite human, no, but close. AI stands for Artificial Intelligence. But, I think that's a conversation for another time. We should focus on the task at hand."

"Sure," she said. "But I don't know how much of this I'll understand."

"I'm going to do what I can to help you understand," said James. "Your idea, it's not a bad one by any means. And it would likely work if our only goal was to prevent the ship from sinking."

She tilted her head. "You mean, it's not?" And then she remembered. "Oh, right… uh, Cillian something, right?" She turned to me—I nodded.

"That's right," said James. "It's a means to an end, really. We want to stop it from sinking, of course, but our primary goal is to save a man on board… the Cillian Hughes you mentioned. He's an Irish scientist who's traveling to America to, like many onboard, start a new life."

"And he's of great importance, I assume?"

"Yes. Through his future breakthrough with nanotechnology, he's going to revolutionize the medical field as we know it. We're talking about ridding the world of any and all diseases, viruses, you name it."

Hanna suddenly sniffed the air inside the lab, her expression returning to one of confusion, or maybe it was of surprise—it was hard to know for sure.

"Everything okay?" I asked.

"I didn't notice until now, but the air here is... I don't know, clean smelling? It's much better than back in my time."

"Yes," said James. "We've come a long way since 1912 in regard to health and safety regulations. In many states, smoking is illegal in all public areas, including restaurants and bars."

"You're joking!"

"Nope. It's helped a great deal with our overall air quality. However, we're still dealing with the adverse effects of burning fossil fuels, but that's yet another conversation for another time. Back to Titanic."

"Wow," she said. "I feel like I'd need to stay here for months to catch up on everything."

James laughed. "Well, you did jump ahead 107 years. Anyway, Cillian Hughes. As I explained to Andrew when I asked him to help with this mission, I discovered an alternate universe where the Titanic doesn't sink, and in this universe there are no remaining illnesses to speak of."

"An alternative universe? What?"

He sighed. "This is going to be hard for you, Hanna, but there are other worlds than this one out there. Most of humanity will only ever know this miniscule speck of the vast universe that we call Earth, however, the truth is there are an infinite number of alternate, or parallel if you like, universes as well. Sometimes similar to ours, other times impossibly different, but they are there nonetheless."

The whole multiverse thing was even hard for me to grasp, even though I had seen it for myself. The idea that at any given moment, in one of these alternate universes, there's a version of you who is doing literally all of the things you've ever thought about doing. Wished you'd been a doctor? There's a version of you out there who is. A version of you who's in jail for murder? Yup, there's one of those, too. It really messes with your head if you think too much about it.

"This is impossible," said Hanna. "How… how did you find this other world?"

"On accident," admitted James. "I was doing some maintenance on the Anode Reactor… the device that makes time travel possible, and I accidentally created a wormhole to a random location in space and time. The odds of such a thing happening again are beyond comprehension."

"Hang on," said Hanna. "What does this have to do with why we can't stop the Titanic from ever sailing that day?"

I chimed in. "Cillian has to complete his voyage to New York precisely as it happened in the alternative universe."

"That's right," said James. "Hanna, are you familiar with the butterfly effect?"

She nodded, although hesitantly. "Andrew explained it a bit to me before we came."

"Well, the science behind it gets complicated, but at its simplest it states that even a miniscule change to something at one point in time can have catastrophic consequences later on. It gets its name from the idea that a butterfly flapping its wings could cause a slight change in air pressure that would lead to a tornado at a later point in time.

"Anyway, that's exactly what we're dealing with here. In the alternate universe, Cillian only has this world-changing breakthrough after he arrived in New York on the Titanic and finds the perfect group of colleagues to help him. If we stop the ship from sailing, even delaying it for an hour or two, we jeopardize the entire timeline."

Hanna let out a heavy sigh as she fell back in her chair. I couldn't have agreed more with her at that point. The more I learned about time travel and all its potential consequences, the more it made me feel guilty about ever wishing to go back in time to experience certain historical events. Despite hearing all this, however, I was still determined to do all I could to save the Titanic.

"Okay," I said. "So, we can't just stop the ship or delay it from sailing. That means it has to be something we do onboard. Oh, by the way James, the coal fire is real. I saw it with my own eyes."

"No kidding?" said James.

"Hang on," said Hanna, perking back up. "A fire? On Titanic?"

"Yeah…" I scratched at the back of my head. "It started back in Belfast."

"How'd it start?"

"Poor coal quality," I said. "During that time there was a massive coal shortage, causing several ships to offload their coal for Titanic to sail."

"How do you know all of this?"

James laughed and left the room for a moment, and upon his return he had a book—my book. He handed it to Hanna.

Her eyes grew as she picked it up. "You wrote a book on the Titanic?"

"Like I told you earlier, I have a fascination with the ship and her story."

She flipped through some of the pages, unsure of how to feel. "This is remarkable."

"It's why I chose him to help with this," said James. "I knew if there was any way this could work, he'd think of it."

"Yeah, as I'm sitting here in your lab asking for help."

James smiled. “Don’t be so hard on yourself. You’ll think of something. What else can we use? You know this maiden voyage better than anyone.”

“Well, my original idea was to intercept the last ice warning they received. It was from the SS Missaba. Rumor has it that this last warning, which was the most vital of them all, never reached Captain Smith… or any of his officers.”

“Why?” asked Hanna, who was now completely invested in the conversation after adjusting to her 2019 surroundings.

I shrugged. “Nobody knows. The only one who would know for sure would be Harold Bride, the wireless operator that night. Anyway, my plan was to gain access to the wireless room, grab this ice warning, and make sure the captain sees it.”

“There’s a ‘but’ coming, right?” said James.

“Yeah, a big one unfortunately. While this plan has a higher chance of success, it’s quite risky. This last ice warning wasn’t received until 9:40 p.m. on the night of the sinking. That means if this plan fails, I’d only have two hours until the Titanic hits the iceberg to come up with an alternative. I don’t like cutting it that close.”

Hanna’s face scrunched up in confusion. “I don’t get it,” she said. “Forgive me, as I obviously don’t understand this time travel stuff at all, but if you have such a device, can’t you try as many times as you need to fix this? Say this ice warning plan fails, just go back and try again.”

I shook my head and motioned to James. “Technically that’s correct,” I said. “But, there’s a serious catch.”

“That’s correct,” said James. “The human body isn’t designed to experience such vast changes in the timeline. Once or twice every now and then doesn’t seem to matter, but the more often a person travels back and forth with the device, their body begins to degrade. The distance traveled, past or future, also makes a difference."

"You know this for certain?" asked Hanna.

His face darkened. "Yes, unfortunately. I can feel it in my bones. I've used the device far too often, and I've gone way too far into both the past and future. I don't believe I'll live much longer… six months, give or take."

Hanna's hand covered her mouth—this action was a common one, as you can imagine. Although, the news about James's prognosis shocked me as well. I remember this conversation as if it just happened yesterday. The effects of persistent time travel on the body were one of the biggest hindrances discovered with this mission. Like Hanna had mentioned, if it weren't for this limitation, I could go back and forth until I managed to save the Titanic (and Cillian). But, James felt the risk wasn't worth it. He had personally experienced the effects, and was now paying with his life.

A long awkward silence followed, one which I finally decided to break. "So, with all that being said, this next trip back has to be the last. Either we find a way to prevent the sinking or bust."

Hanna sighed and leaned against her arm on the table. "Surely you have other ideas, Andrew. You said it yourself… you know pretty much everything there is to know about Titanic. How about in your book? Maybe if we look through it we'll see something."

See something… look… the lookout… crows nest, binoculars! That's it! I thought as one of my previous ideas came back to the forefront of my mind.

"Hanna, you're brilliant!" I said.

She blushed. "What'd I say?"

"James, I think I've got it. Can you get me a pair of binoculars from 1912? Ones that would have been used on Titanic?"

He thought it over for a moment. "Yes, I think so. I can have Anansi go back through a wormhole and grab a pair."

"What will that do for us?" asked Hanna.

I took a moment to calm myself down—the more I thought about this plan, the more I thought it would work, which was getting me excited.

"It's a long story, but due to several unfortunate events, second officer David Blair was demoted and asked to leave the ship at Southampton. This wouldn't have been an issue, save for the fact Blair had the key to the locker where the lookout's binoculars were stored. He left in such a hurry he forgot to give the key to another officer."

Understanding began to show on Hanna's face. "You're going to bring them a pair of binoculars! And with your master engineer cover, they won't suspect anything. That could work!"

James nodded. "I agree. That's a good plan, Andrew. And you can fall back on the ice warning plan as well."

"Right. This plan easily has the highest chance of success. While being questioned in the British inquiry after the sinking, lookout Fred fleet testified that had they had binoculars, he would have certainly seen the iceberg soon enough for the Titanic to avoid it."

James stood up. "Sounds like a plan to me. I'll work with Anansi to get the binoculars so we can get you two back to 1912."

It took the two of them less than half an hour to traverse a wormhole back to 1912, grab a pair of binoculars identical to the ones used on Titanic, and return to James's lab. His resourcefulness never ceased to amaze me. Not long after,

Hanna and I were standing on the same platform we'd arrived on.

"One more thing," said James, handing me the binoculars. "While I agree this plan seems simple enough and should work, remember, the past doesn't want to be changed. It will fight you every step of the way. Just something to keep in mind."

I nodded. "Thanks, James. Hopefully the next time I see you, the Titanic didn't sink."

He smiled and initialized the Anode Reactor. "Safe travels."

A moment later we arrived back to the same moment, down to the millisecond, we had originally left. As the two of us once again stood in cabin C-73, binoculars in my hand, I felt a sense of optimism. I had three days, twelve hours to prevent the worst maritime disaster in history—and for the first time since boarding Titanic, I felt I could.

CHAPTER VIII

1

As with any historical event, Titanic had her share of conspiracy theories. One of the more outlandish being that she didn't actually sink at all. It was theorized to have been her sister ship, Olympic, that hit the iceberg on the night of April 14th. A number of arguments have been made in favor of this switch happening, all of which have since been debunked. But if you know anything about conspiracy theorists, once they get it in their head that it happened how they think it did, there's no convincing them otherwise. I won't bother you with all of the countless claims and how they've been debunked, but I'll share one.

This theory rests primarily on an attempted insurance scam made by the White Star Line. After the RMS Olympic collided with the HMS Hawk (yes, this event really did happen), the damage to Titanic's sister ship was thought to have been much greater than was released publicly. This claim, combined with another claim of Titanic's insurance being raised considerably just five days before her maiden voyage, made it plausible (at least to these theorists) that they had switched the two ships in order to receive a large insurance payout after deliberately sinking one of their ocean liners.

This claim is one of the easiest to debunk. This insurance increase simply didn't happen. Lloyds Maritime Insurance, which was the company used by White Star to insure their ships (at least partially, more to come in the paragraphs below), provided records that showed the Titanic was actually under-insured ($5,000,000) in relation to how much a total loss would cost (roughly $7,500,000).

To further show how ridiculous this claim was, White Star actually insured the remaining damage of their ships (up to $600,000). So, if this switch had happened and Olympic ("Titanic") was purposely sunk for the insurance payout, White Star would have had to cover even more out of their own pockets. It just doesn't make financial sense, and therefore would not have been something the company would have done. The wreck at the bottom of the Atlantic is the Titanic, not Olympic.

2

As Hanna sat on the bed, taking in everything that just happened, I began to realize she may have been better off without my intervention. Sure, she's likely destined to go down with the ship, but thanks to me she now has to try and mentally grasp the idea of not only time travel being real but also the idea of multiple universes existing. That'd be a tall order for anyone, regardless of what time period you're from.

I sat down beside her on the bed, putting my hand on her leg. "I'm sorry for getting you into this."

She turned and met my gaze. "Don't be sorry. I'd much rather try to comprehend time travel than spend my days as a prisoner and stowaway."

That's fair.

"Besides," she continued, standing up and twirling in her dress. "Thanks to you, I'm now a first class passenger with an entire wardrobe of proper dresses!" She came back to me and hugged me tightly. "Let's take another walk. You can drop off the binoculars on the way, too."

I thought about declining, but I knew she was right. Some fresh air would do us both good. But, I had to know her thoughts on what just happened. "You sure are taking time travel pretty well, all things considered. Are you doing okay?"

She shrugged. "Honestly, I'm trying not to think of it too much. Taking me back to your time was quite an experience, one I'm sure I won't ever forget, but I think it's best if I just let you handle the situation."

That wasn't the response I had been expecting, but then again I'm not sure what exactly I was expecting. She's just trying to enjoy her time in the present, and who can argue with her on that.

"Good enough for me. Oh, and don't forget we have dinner at 6:30 tonight as well."

She had. "Oh my, that's right. Who will be there again?"

"Thomas Andrews, the chief designer of Titanic, Captain Smith, and a few of the other officers. I imagine Charles Lightoller and William Murdoch, but I'm not certain."

"Are you sure you want me there? It seems much too formal."

I kissed her cheek. "Nonsense. Of course I want you there,

but only if you want to go. I won't try and force you to do anything."

She smiled and kissed me on the lips. "You're sweet, Andrew. I'll be there. Come on, let's head up to the Boat Deck."

"One more thing," I said, grabbing the binoculars. "For reasons I'm sure you can understand, we can't discuss any of what just happened outside this cabin."

"Of course," she said, taking hold of my hand. "I can't imagine the impact of something like that."

"We'd both end up where you were headed the night we met, and we'd meet our ends in the icy waters of the Atlantic."

3

I decided to wait on giving the binoculars to the lookouts. Hanna and I enjoyed another walk around the Boat Deck, taking in the beautiful weather the afternoon had to offer. It was clear and calm—the water was like glass, other than the wake created by Titanic slicing through it. During our walk we ran into First Officer Murdoch, who greeted us with a wave and a passing comment about seeing us at dinner tonight.

William McMaster Murdoch, born in Scotland in 1873, was the officer in charge on the night of the sinking. In two separate films about the Titanic, Murdoch is portrayed shooting passengers and himself during the sinking. This was based on several eyewitness testimonies of a shooting/suicide by an officer during the launching of the last lifeboat. It's possible he was the officer they saw. There's no evidence that proves he was, but there's no evidence that proves he wasn't, either.

After getting in another few laps around the Boat Deck, Hanna and I returned to our respective cabins to get ready for dinner that evening. I opened my suitcase and looked through the bespoke suits provided by James, struggling to decide which to wear. The one I'd been wearing since I boarded was great, but it was time for a change. Towards the bottom I found the perfect suit for the occasion. It was a black tail coat, complete with satin faced lapels, a white undershirt and waistcoat, and a pair of freshly shined black dress shoes. I felt more dapper than I'd ever felt before—and I loved it.

4

We got to the Dining Saloon just before half past six that evening. As we entered, we were immediately greeted by Mr. Andrews, who was also dressed in a black tail coat.

"Ah, Mr. Lawson," he said, holding out his hand. "So glad you could join us."

I shook his hand. "Wouldn't miss it, Mr. Andrews." I turned to Hanna. "Hanna, this is Thomas Andrews, chief designer of Titanic. Mr. Andrews, this is Hanna. She's… a friend." I felt myself blushing but didn't know what else to say.

He smiled. "No need to be discreet with me, Mr. Lawson. It's none of my business either way. Nice to meet you, miss." He bowed slightly. "Shall we join the others?"

I nodded. "Yes, of course."

We followed him to the table. I took Hanna's hand and gave her a *sorry* look, but she smiled and waved it away. I felt her squeeze my hand as we got to the table. It was a long rectangular table covered in a crisp white cloth, and on that sat the finest china I'd ever seen. I pushed in Hanna's chair after she sat down, and then took my seat next to her. Also at the table was Captain Smith, Bruce Ismay, Thomas Andrews, Charles Lightoller, and William Murdoch. Everyone I had expected, save for Mr. Ismay.

"Very good of you to join us, Mr. Lawson," said Smith, holding up his glass of (I assumed) scotch. "And who's the lovely lady by your side?"

Hanna was blushing but also smiling. "This is Hanna," I said. "On our first day at sea she was lost so I helped her find her way about the ship. Hopefully it's okay for her to join." I know, I know, I lied to the Captain. Sue me again. I just hoped Thomas wouldn't say anything.

"Of course," said Smith. "Welcome, Hanna. Please, both of you, get yourselves a drink. Dinner will be served at seven."

I ordered a gin and tonic, while Hanna stuck with her red wine. Dinner was served promptly at seven, and it was some of the best food I'd ever tasted. I had a leg of lamb in a mint sauce, along with roasted squash and potatoes. For dessert I had something called Waldorf pudding. I'd never heard of it, but it was delicious. It had vanilla pudding, nutmeg, and roasted diced apples. By the time I finished I was stuffed. So much so that my suit felt just a bit tighter than when I had arrived.

There was some talking about this and that after dinner, but nothing noteworthy that I can recall. Around 8:15, Hanna and I excused ourselves and returned to my cabin. We spent the remainder of the evening talking about our lives before Titanic. It made me wonder if there could be something between the two of us. *How would that work? Either way, one of us would have to leave not just their home, but their timeline.* This was a question I didn't have an answer for, at least not yet.

"Could you see us being more than friends?" asked Hanna. "I know the situation is… unusual, but I'm okay with that."

"But you've only known me for two days. And during those days I've already lied to you about who I really am."

She waved this away. "I understand why you did it. Not exactly something you can easily bring up in conversation."

"I do like you, Hanna, really." I sighed. "I think I should focus on doing what needs to be done here onboard. Once that gets sorted, then the two of us can decide how to proceed. Fair?"

She nodded and leaned over and kissed me on the lips. "Very fair." She wrapped her arm around me. "Come on, let's lay down for the night."

And so marked the end of my second night aboard Titanic. I was really enjoying my time with Hanna, and I hoped it would never end. My plan for tomorrow was to take the binoculars to the lookouts first thing in the morning. Afterward, I needed to make sure I had a solid backup plan in place. James's last words to me about the past fighting back was echoing in my mind as I felt my eyelids getting heavy.

We both slept.

5

2 days, 15 hours, 40 minutes until disaster

I awoke at eight the next morning with Hanna cuddled up to me, still sound asleep. We had been up late enjoying one another—I'll leave it at that. While part of me was saying just stay in bed all day with Hanna, the responsible part of me said I should have been up an hour ago. Thankfully, I listened to the latter and quietly got myself out of bed. My plan for the morning was to give the binoculars to the lookouts. With any luck, they wouldn't be too suspicious and accept them without question. I was banking on my badge to help with this. After washing my face and putting on a pair of slacks and a more casual dress shirt, I kissed Hanna on the cheek and headed out of the cabin.

A few minutes later I was staring up at the ladder inside the forward mast, leading to the crow's nest. The Titanic had six lookouts, with two being on duty at all times. It was Frederick Fleet and Reginald Lee who were on duty the night Titanic hit the iceberg, and coincidentally, it was the same two lookouts that were on duty that morning. I did my best not to startle them as I announced my presence.

"Good morning up there," I said to the men. "My name is Andrew Lawson. One of you mind coming down for a moment?"

"Mr. Lawson? The master engineer?"

I guess the word has spread throughout all of the crew.

"The very same," I said. "Is that you, Mr. Fleet?"

"Aye. Coming down now, sir."

A moment later I was face-to-face with Frederick himself. Born in England, he was twenty-four at the time of Titanic's maiden voyage. He would go on to survive the sinking, and would marry his wife Eva in 1917. After Titanic, Fleet would leave White Star, instead sailing for Union-Castle until 1936, when he came ashore to work as a ship builder for none other than Harland and Wolf. Unfortunately, in 1964 his wife would pass away. Immediately after, his brother-in-law (with whom they lived) kicked him out, and Fleet subsequently hung himself.

All of these facts raced through my mind as the man stood

before me, a healthy twenty-four-year-old. It was one of the few downsides of being on the ship—knowing the (more often than not) tragic futures of the people I encountered. Regardless, I had a job here to do. Perhaps if the Titanic survives its maiden voyage, life for Fleet will be different. Time is a strange beast.

Fred stood at attention. "Good morning, sir. What can I do for you?"

I put out my hand in a *that's not necessary* motion. "At ease, Mr. Fleet. And, good morning to you as well. How are things up top?"

He relaxed, but only a little. "All is fine this morning, sir. Lee and I just relieved the night crew about an hour ago."

"Glad to hear it," I said, pulling out the binoculars. "Would you have any use for a pair of these?" I handed them to Fleet.

His eyes widened. "Blimey, you must have read our minds. We was just talking, Lee and I, about how the officers hadn't given us any binoculars." He hesitantly took them from me and put out his other hand. "Much obliged, sir. I will make sure to put these to good use."

I shook his hand. "You're welcome, Mr. Fleet. And make sure you do just that. I have a bad feeling about upcoming ice in a day or two."

"Aye," he said. "The nights have been getting colder. We're approaching the ice fields. Anyway, I should get back up top. Thanks again for these, sir." I nodded and turned away as he climbed the ladder back up to the crow's nest.

Okay, so maybe the ice comment was a little on the nose, but I couldn't help saying it. Now that Fred had the binoculars, all I could do was wait. With any luck I had just changed the fate of the Titanic. Unfortunately, James's last words about the past still lived rent free in my mind. *The past doesn't want to be changed.* For all I know, Fred dropped the binoculars as he was making his way back up the ladder. I should have told him to be careful with them, but I felt that went without saying.

6

After meeting with Fleet, I contemplated what to do next. I felt somewhat helpless as all I could do was wait—wait until the iceberg was spotted. A pit formed in my stomach at the thought of that. Could I really just sit around and wait for the ship to be so close to peril? *Hang on*, I thought. *Something bad happens today, doesn't it? Hmm, maybe it's tomorrow.* I dug through my memory, trying to remember what it was. *The Wireless Room*, it finally came. *Ah, but that happens on the 13th, not the 12th.* Regardless, I decided to stop in and visit. Perhaps something would come of it that would help the situation.

The Marconi Wireless Room, named after the company (*The Marconi Wireless Telegraph Company of America*) who owned and installed its equipment, was where wireless operators Jack Phillips and Harold Bride sent and received messages between ships and shore over a Marconi transmitter. These communications were done via Morse code—'dots and dashes'. Not that you asked, or likely care, but the distress call of 'SOS' transmitted in Morse code would be '...____...". When Titanic's purser brought messages from the passengers, it was Jack and Harold's job to send them onward to shore. They would also receive messages from other ships, most of which were ice warnings.

The Marconi Room was located on the Boat Deck, just aft of the Officer's Promenade, which was off-limits to regular passengers. Fortunately, I was far from a regular passenger. I knocked on the door before letting myself in. Admittedly, I was starting to get used to my unrestricted access to the ship. As I entered, Harold Bride turned to acknowledge me. He immediately recognized who I was and stood at attention.

"Morning, sir," he said. "I had heard a master engineer was onboard. It's a pleasure, if I may say so, sir."

While I was getting used to the unrestricted access, I didn't think I'd ever get used to the level of respect shown to me by the crew (and by everyone, really).

I smiled and put out my hand. "My name is Andrew Lawson." He happily shook my hand before returning to his rigid stance. "Please, relax Mr. Bride." It was the same as with Mr. Fleet.

It looked physically painful to him, but he managed to relax. "Something I can do for you, Mr. Lawson?"

I shook my head. "Just was in the area and wanted to have a look at the wireless setup onboard."

Bride's eyes lit up. "Oh, well I'd be glad to show you, sir. Are you familiar with Morse code?" I saw a hint of embarrassment on his face. "Of course you are. Apologies, sir."

I laughed and put my hand on his shoulder. "Mr. Bride, I really need you to relax. I'm not here on any special assignment or anything of the sort. We're just two men talking, yeah?" He nodded. "Good. But yes, I do know Morse code, although I don't think it's a common thing to know, so you were right to ask." I finally saw him relax to the point he almost appeared his normal self.

"Anything you'd specifically like to see?" he asked. "I do have quite a number of passenger messages to send, if you'd like to see how that is done."

I was well aware of how sending and receiving messages over the Marconi transmitter worked, but I agreed to watch nevertheless. This would give me a good reason to ask Bride about any ice warnings they've received, as well as the incident that's going to happen tomorrow night.

Late on April 13th, around eleven p.m., Phillips noticed the system starting to give him trouble, eventually it would stop working altogether. Bride is called out of bed to assist with repairing the system. A short in one of the transformers would turn out to be the cause, however, it would take the two operators until five the next morning to repair it. Six hours with no way to send or receive messages. Were there ice warnings within that timeframe that could have made a difference? That's what I was hoping to find out.

Bride had just finished forwarding two more passenger messages when several more came through the receiving pipe of the wireless room.

"Never a shortage of messages," he said, grabbing the messages from their basket. "Anything else I can do for you, Mr. Lawson? I really should focus on getting the rest of these sent out."

I knew my time was quickly running out, so I decided to take a chance with Bride. He was, after all, not technically employed by White Star, but by Marconi. Still, the conversation could have ended poorly for me. It was worth the risk, though. At the last second, I decided to make up a lie instead. In hindsight, I'm glad I went this route.

"There is, actually. Two things. I was recently on another ship that used Marconi transmitters, the SS Birma, and their operator had a terrible time when one of the transformers had a short in it. Took the poor lad hours to get it back online."

Mr. Bride's eyes widened. "No kidding, sir?" I nodded. "I'd sure hate for us to be in a jam like that… Phillips and I have our hands full with all these passenger messages to send out."

"I couldn't agree more. How about once Mr. Phillips wakes up, the two of you do an inspection of the transformers to make sure they're all in working order."

He nodded, taking a card and making a note of this so as not to forget about it amongst all the messages he still had to send. "That sounds like a great idea, sir. I'm writing a note now."

"Good." I was relieved that this lie had worked.

He hesitated before speaking again. "You said there were two things, sir?"

"Yes," I said. "It may likely prove to be more important than the first."

He sighed and grabbed another message card to take down a second note. "Let's have it then."

I liked this response. It showed that he was getting more comfortable around me—that was good. While some officers would likely have frowned upon such a tone, I appreciated the camaraderie.

"I've gotten word that an abundance of ice has been reported in a region we'll be going through. I want you and Phillips to make sure you pay close attention to any ice warnings that come in."

He started writing and then stopped, looking up at me. "What's so important about that? Ice in the Atlantic, as well as receiving ice warnings from other ships are both commonplace in this line of work, sir."

"Yes, of course. But, from what I was told, the amount of ice was most unusual. I'm not an expert by any means, but something about the Labrador current and how much farther south it has been drifting this year is causing ice bergs to also be pushed into our path. Just keep a sharper ear for any ice warnings, yeah?"

Mr. Bride scribbled the rest of what I'd said onto the card and then looked back up at me.

"Okay, noted. I appreciate you letting me know. "

I smiled and got up from the chair next to him. "No problem at all, Mr. Bride. I care a lot about this ship, and I want her maiden voyage to go smoothly." I pointed to his notes. "Don't forget about those… it's very important you don't."

I patted him on the shoulder as I left the wireless room and arrived back onto the Boat Deck. As I made my way back towards C Deck, I felt a wave of bittersweet emotions flood over me. On one hand, I had two plans in place to prevent the Titanic from hitting the iceberg. And I had a last resort plan c, but I didn't want to think about that right now. But, at the same time, all I could do now was wait. I felt hopeless, hopeful, sad, happy, uncertain, and relieved, all at the same time.

I needed a drink.

CHAPTER IX

1

Another factor that is thought to have contributed to Titanic hitting the iceberg was the size of her rudder. It was said to have been too small for a ship of her size. For those unfamiliar, a rudder is part of the steering apparatus on a ship that is fastened outside the hull, usually at the stern. It operates on the principle of unequal water pressures. When the rudder is turned so that one side is more exposed to the force of the water flowing past it than the other side, the stern will be thrust away from the side that the rudder is on and the boat will swerve from its original course. In other words, if you turn a rudder to port, the bow will turn to port while the stern will turn to starboard, and vice-versa. Think of it like backing up a car and how you'd turn the wheel in that situation.

Now that we're up to speed on what a rudder is, was

Titanic's rudder too small? Very technically (I won't be including the math), yes, however, the difference between its size and the size it should have been is miniscule. Because of this, I don't believe this played any part in the disaster. What did, however, was the commands given to the engine room for all stop, and then full astern immediately after the iceberg was spotted. This sudden change in the flow of water passing over the rudder significantly lowered its efficiency, and therefore limited how quickly the ship could turn. It's believed by some that if the only change made after spotting the iceberg was to turn the ship to port, she would have not hit the iceberg.

This isn't a fact, of course. The problem with this theory (as well as most of the ones surrounding Titanic) is that we have (very) limited first-hand testimonies to work off of, and even some of those are conflicting with one another. Because of this, people have crafted hundreds of their own theories, based on what was said under oath at the US and British inquiries after the sinking. I'm simply a history teacher with a love for the Titanic, who is telling his story of being hurled back in time to try and prevent the very thing I'd spent more than ten years of my life researching.

More than once I'd wondered about that paradox. If I managed to stop the Titanic from sinking, and also made it back to 2019, what would I replace that semester with? Usually it was devoted to the Titanic disaster. I suppose it's best not to dwell on that line of thinking for too long, especially when you as the reader are certainly ready to get back to 1912.

Let's do that now.

2

After doing my very best at lying, in an effort to warn Mr. Bride of Titanic's impending doom, I fulfilled my need for a drink via the smoking room. I considered asking Hanna if she wanted to get breakfast together, but I needed some time to myself first. I didn't like how I was feeling that morning, and despite thinking it would help, the alcohol was only worsening my mood. *Maybe this is the work of the past,* I thought. *This is its way of preventing me from changing it.* I finished my third glass of bourbon, shook myself off, and headed down to my cabin to meet Hanna. Perhaps her company was what I actually needed.

That indeed turned out to be what I needed. Hanna and I got breakfast together, and I told her about my busy morning. She asked me if I thought either plan would work, and I told her the truth.

"I'd be lying if I said I was confident of either plan. In literally any other circumstance, I would say yes, however, the past is working against me here." I took another sip of coffee. "But I sure hope one of them works."

She smiled, that beautiful smile I was growing more and more fond of. "It'll work, I know it. If there's anyone who can save this ship, it's you, Andrew."

Hanna really was something else. Just a few minutes of being with her had completely changed my mood. My mind felt clearer, and I even had more optimism than before. *At least one of the plans will work,* I thought. *One will work.*

"Would you like to go to the Turkish bath with me today?" I asked, finishing the rest of my coffee. "I've always wanted to experience it, especially after reading so much about them over the years."

"Oh, that would be wonderful! I never thought I'd be able to take part in something like that, and certainly not with a master engineer such as yourself." She nudged my foot underneath the table and winked at me. "Kidding aside, I must say once again how grateful I am for everything. Thank you." She put her hand on mine. It was nice.

"You're very welcome, Hanna." I took a glance at the time —10:45. "Shall we go change and head to the bath?"

She nodded and we both got up and left for our cabins.

3

The remainder of Friday was, for the most part, uneventful. Hanna and I had a great and relaxing time at the Turkish bath. Afterward we got changed and spent a few hours in the smoking room, enjoying drinks together. I know what you're thinking, and no, neither of us are alcoholics. Despite its grandeur, there really weren't an abundance of things to do onboard Titanic. Unlike the massive cruise liners back in 2019, for the ocean liners of 1912 it was more about basking in the luxury that the ships provided as opposed to having activities to constantly fill your time.

While in the smoking room, Mr. Andrews joined us for a few drinks. He talked at length about how great the maiden voyage had been thus far, and he was adamant that we tell him straight away if something isn't to our liking while onboard. I had always read about the man's level-headed attitude, and his near constant attempts to help people when he could, but experiencing it first-hand was another matter entirely. I strived to be more like him in my everyday life.

Later we took lunch again in the Cafe Parisian. It was busy this time, with nearly every table occupied. As we were eating, I happened to notice a familiar looking man at the table next to us. I realized who it was, and tried to look away before he met my gaze, but it was too late. Cillian Hughes was staring back at me. *Damn,* I thought. *Gotta be careful.*

"Good afternoon, sir," he said, his heavy Irish accent unmistakeable. "I'm Cillian, Cillian Hughes." He put out his hand.

I reluctantly shook his hand and smiled. "Nice to meet you, I'm Andrew Lawson. This is my lady, Hanna." I stopped pretending that she was just a friend, which made her blush at the moment. "How's the trip been for you?" I would have preferred the interaction to have ended there, but I couldn't help myself.

"Oh, quite fine, thank you. Titanic is quite the ship."

I nodded in agreement. "She sure is. Well, enjoy your—"

"What do you do for work, Mr. Lawson?" he interrupted.

I knew at that point it was a mistake to keep talking to him, but I wasn't one to be rude.

"I'm a master engineer," I said, pulling the badge out of my pocket and showing it to him. I had stopped wearing it around my neck after the second day as the crew all seemed to know who I was.

"Blimey, a master engineer huh? I bet that's quite a way to make a livin'." He took another quick bite of his sandwich. "I'm a medical man myself. Yes sir, going to America in hopes of starting my own practice."

And redefine how we treat diseases throughout the world, I thought. *Assuming this butterfly hasn't already flapped its wings and ruined everything.*

I smiled politely. "Well, Hanna and I must be going," I said, standing up. Thankfully, I saw Hanna stand as well, apparently understanding my concern. "I wish you the best with your medical endeavors, Mr. Hughes."

He reached for my hand again. "Thank you very much, sir. I hope to help as many as I can. Good day to you both!"

Once we were out of the Cafe and earshot, Hanna stopped me. I could tell by her expression that she remembered the discussion on the butterfly effect.

"Was that bad?" she asked. "I could tell you weren't comfortable with the conversation, and that's unusual for you."

I ran my hands through my hair, uncertain of what to think. "Well, it wasn't good. This is exactly the kind of thing they were talking about when naming the butterfly effect." I sighed. "Nothing we can do about it now." I took out my watch, which told me it was half past one. "I better go up top and check on my plans. Let's meet up later, yeah?"

She smiled and kissed me on the lips. "Of course. I actually made friends with the lady who was nice enough to give me these dresses, and we're planning to meet for tea."

"No kidding? That's some high class company there." We both chuckled. I hugged her tightly and kissed her again. "Have a good time. Hope to see you for dinner."

We parted ways just outside the Cafe—me going up to the Boat Deck and Hanna to meet her friend for tea.

Up on the Boat Deck, I managed to catch Fleet still on duty. He thanked me again for the binoculars and mentioned they were the nicest pair he'd ever seen. I was relieved to hear that, at least so far, the past wasn't trying to intervene with my plan(s) to change it.

I found the same was true in the wireless room. Phillips and Bride did in fact find a faulty portion in one of the transformers. It took them a couple hours but they got it fixed. Two for two with my plans to stop the ship from sinking. Like I briefly mentioned before, I had a plan c in the back of my mind, but that was going to be a very last resort, for reasons I won't go into here.

4

Friday evening was filled with more food, more alcohol, and later that night, more intimacy between Hanna and me. I called her 'babe' for the first time that night. It was just after we finished. We were cuddling in my bed and it just slipped out. She kissed my lips passionately and snuggled up against my chest. That night was the happiest I'd been in many years.

A few hours later, as Hanna was sleeping on my chest, I found myself lying awake, worrying about the coming events. Tomorrow—well, I had actually noticed it was near one a.m., so it was now the 13th. So, tomorrow (the 14th) would be the day disaster was to strike in the form of a colossal iceberg. I did some quick math—roughly 1 day, 22 hours, and 44 minutes until Titanic would strike the iceberg. I felt another pit forming in my stomach, knowing how bad things could get in the coming hours, and feeling helpless with nothing to do but wait.

After a few more minutes of worrying, I felt my eyes starting to get heavy. I finally managed to sleep at just after two.

5

I awoke at seven a.m. to the sound of Hanna washing off her face over the sink. She was still in her nightgown, which was purple and made of silk—it really was quite lovely. She smiled as she turned and saw I was awake.

"Good morning, dear," she said, coming back to join me

in bed. She was babe and I was dear. *I could get used to this,* I thought. "How'd you sleep?"

I yawned and stretched. "I slept well, although it took me quite a while to fall asleep."

She nodded her understanding. "You're worried your plans will fail, aren't you?"

"Of course," I said. "What if I can't stop it from sinking?"

She wrapped her arms around me, which immediately made me feel better. "You'll find a way. But, if for some reason you don't, then we'll do whatever necessary to survive. We'll use your time travel thing and you can take me back to live in your time."

I had thought of this possibility, of course, but I hadn't mentioned it to Hanna at all. I had no doubts about wanting to spend the rest of my life with this woman, but could she make it okay in 2019? To say things were different was quite obviously an understatement. Also, what about those 1,500 souls on board that would perish? Could I live with myself knowing I failed to prevent their deaths?

"Andrew? You okay?"

I realized I was zoning out, so I forced myself to focus. "Yeah, sorry… just thinking about life with you in 2019."

"And?"

"I think it would be great. Challenging for you at first, but I think you'd figure it out soon enough, especially with me to help."

She smiled and kissed me. "See? All settled then. Absolute worst case, if the Titanic isn't saveable, we can escape to 2019."

As I sat there, Hanna's arms wrapped around me, I wondered if I could really do that—just give up on Titanic so easily. My plan c would work, I knew it would, but it came with great risk—would surely jeopardize the future we were actively discussing. *I'll make that choice when and if I have to.*

"How about some breakfast," I said, running my hands through Hanna's hair, its golden red hue shining in the light of my cabin.

"Yes, please. I'm starving!"

6

My Saturday onboard was even less eventful than Friday. Like I mentioned previously, there wasn't a vast amount of things to do, but we still made the most of it. More food, more drinks, and more of everything that I've already told you about. We had breakfast, followed by a few trips around the Boat Deck. The views from there really were breathtaking—like nothing I'd ever seen before. We ran into Captain Smith, who was having a cup of tea and looking out across the ocean. We spoke briefly before continuing on our way.

Lunch was more sandwiches and a cup or two of coffee. We ran into the older couple I had met on my first day onboard—Mr. and Mrs Baxter. I introduced them to Hanna and her to them. They told me all about their lovely time onboard, and how much they were looking forward to seeing New York for the first time. I felt a wrenching of my heart, knowing there was a chance they'd never make it, but I tried to not let this feeling show externally.

After lunch we did our own thing for a few hours, which had become our routine. Hanna was getting rather friendly with Mrs Aster, the woman who'd given her the wardrobe filled with dresses. And yes, this was *the* Mrs Astor, married to John Jacob Astor IV, the richest man in the world at the time. Hanna and Madeleine started meeting for tea around one p.m. to chat about who knows what, but I was happy they were getting on so well.

In the meantime, I followed up again with the lookouts in the crow's nest as well as Phillips and Bride in the wireless room. So far, all was well. Just over twenty-four hours until the iceberg would be spotted, and at the moment my plans were both safely in place. Even so, I couldn't help but feel a sense of dread deep within myself. I shook it off and made my way to the library to catch up on some reading. I lost track of time, deep in the pages of some novel I can't recall at the moment, and when I next looked at my watch I saw it was five p.m.

A few moments later, I returned to my cabin and met Hanna there, who had been waiting for me.

"There you are," she said, running up and hugging me. "Where have you been?"

"Sorry babe, I was reading in the library. Is everything okay?"

"Fine," she said. "I was just worried is all. I don't like being apart for long anymore."

I shared this feeling, too. Since Hanna and I had gotten closer, she was all I could think about. Never did I think someone could pull my attention away from being onboard the Titanic, but here she was. Granted, I still would catch myself in awe at a certain part of the ship, whether it was the ever beautiful grand staircase or the gorgeous stained glass of the Turkish bath, but overall I was more taken aback by how attracted I was to Hanna. I wanted to be with her and only her.

"Sorry to worry you," I said, kissing her on the lips. "Shall we get ready for dinner?"

"I'm ready," she said. "Was here waiting on you." She playfully poked at me. "Hurry up and change."

After I put on a new suit, this one a deep blue, we went and had dinner, this time just the two of us. We'd often been having meals with Mr. Andrews and/or other members of the crew.

That evening we spent some time together in the library, each getting lost in our own novels. It was late by the time we got back to my cabin. In hindsight, it was rather useless to get Hanna her own cabin—she spent most of her time in mine, which I greatly preferred, by the way.

It was after midnight when I finally felt my eyes getting heavy again. Hanna had passed out over an hour ago. After reading we went to the smoking room and shared a few (too many) drinks. She was stumbling on her way back to the cabin, and was asleep not long after getting into bed.

Today is the day, I thought, lying in bed next to Hanna, listening to her lightly snore. In roughly twenty-three hours, Titanic would collide with the iceberg, and then two hours and forty minutes later, she'd sink to the bottom of the Atlantic. I'd been on board the ship for four days now, and it felt like so much longer—but it went by fast, too. Funny how that seems to happen.

I knew I should sleep. Today would be the longest and most stressful day by far, but every time I began to doze off an intrusive thought brought me back out of it. *I can't do this. What if I fail? What if something happens to Hanna? What if we can't make it back to 2019? Am I going to die here?* These thoughts went on and on for at least another hour. Finally, I became too exhausted to continue thinking, and sleep took me.

CHAPTER X

1

One more strike against the Titanic occurred on the very day she struck the iceberg. April 14th was a Sunday, and church services were held onboard. Captain Smith, who was a strong believer in his faith, conducted the service in the First Class Dining Room. While this in itself wasn't a problem, what made it one was the fact that a lifeboat drill had been scheduled during this same time, and Smith chose to attend the former, canceling the drill.

It's unclear why Smith didn't ask that the drill be rescheduled, but what is clear is that the absence of this drill would lend to the officers being unprepared for the disaster to come later that night. There's no way to prove for certain that this contributed to any specific deaths, but it's safe to say the drill being canceled certainly meant the officers would be slower to react in the event of an emergency.

2

Another fact about the night she sank—the closest ship, the Californian, was a mere ten miles away. Actually, there is debate over just how far away she was—some say ten miles while others say twenty or thirty. Regardless, she was by far the closest to Titanic that night, and could have easily reached her before she sank. Unfortunately, the ship failed to act on Titanic's distress calls. The reasons behind this inaction have been heavily debated ever since. Like many of these "facts", we may never know the actual truth behind it, but we have theories.

The most agreed upon is that the Californian had stopped her engines for the night due to large amounts of ice (there's irony in there somewhere). And unlike Titanic, she only had one wireless operator, who at the time the Titanic hit the iceberg had turned in for the night.

Another theory, which also mentions the Californian stopping for the night, contributes the radio silence to a brief argument between the two wireless operators. Mr. Phillips, the operator of the Titanic, had been trying to catch up on sending passenger messages while they were in range of Cape Race when the operator from the Californian interrupted him with a powerful signal—it was a message warning of nearby ice. Phillips is quoted to have said: "Keep out; shut up, I am working Cape Race!". After this, it's believed the other radio operator turned in for the night, leaving Titanic on her own.

3

The next morning I awoke to a knock at the door. As I rolled out of bed, with Hanna still fast asleep, I checked my watch and saw it was just after six. *That explains my exhaustion,* I thought. I'd only been asleep for four hours. I threw on my robe and opened the door.

It was my steward, Smethells.

"Sorry to wake you, sir." He handed me a silver tray, on it a small envelope, used for carrying messages. "An important message from Mr. Bride. He said to deliver it at once."

I grabbed the envelope from the tray, knowing full well what it said. I thanked Smethells, and told him there was no need to apologize. He bowed slightly and left, closing the door behind him.

"Who was that?" asked Hanna, rubbing her eyes as she was just waking up.

"Smethells, my steward… gave me a message from the wireless room."

I sat down at the table and took the message out of the envelope. It was only three small sentences, but it was enough to tell me that the past was onto me.

Mr. Lawson,

You were right, the wireless system went out again this morning. It's worse than before, and I'm not sure if we'll get it back online before New York. Thought you should know.

-Bride

I remained motionless with the message in my hand for a moment, trying to take in the reality of what this meant. By the sounds of it, Titanic wouldn't be receiving any ice warnings at all today. *At least I still had the binoculars to fall back on.* Although, I had a bad feeling about those as well. I needed to go talk to Mr. Bride.

"Is everything okay?" asked Hanna. She stood behind me, her arms hanging over my shoulders. "What'd the message say?"

I sighed. "The wireless system is down. Sounds like it's pretty bad."

She inhaled sharply. "It's just like you said… it's the past, right? It knows you're trying to change it."

I nodded. "Yes, and it isn't too happy about it." I got up from the chair and faced her. "I have to go… there are things I need to do."

"I know," she said, a sense of sadness appearing in her voice. "It happens tonight, yes?"

"Not as long as I'm onboard." I kissed her on the lips and hugged her tightly. As I pulled away, I noticed the color had slightly drained from her face—she was paler than usual. "Are you feeling okay, babe?"

She forced a smile. "Oh, I'm fine, just a headache is all. Probably too much wine last night." She chuckled, also forced. "Go on and do what you need to. We can meet up for breakfast later."

I nodded and smiled back at her, although not completely convinced. Unfortunately, I had to focus on Titanic right now. I threw on a suit and left the cabin for the Boat Deck.

There was no time to waste.

4

As soon as I entered the wireless room, I immediately noticed both Phillips and Bride frantically working on the system's hardware. I was also greeted with the unmistakable smell of fried electronics. *This is bad.* If one of the primary transformers suffered a short, it would mean disaster. A moment later, Bride noticed me and came out of "the silent room" to greet me.

For those wondering, the silent room was the name given to the room where the Marconi's main transmitter and switch equipment were stored. This transmitter, due to its immense power output (for the time, anyway), would generate a substantially loud hum while in operation. Think of that buzz you sometimes hear when you walk underneath power lines—it's essentially the same thing, only much louder due to the proximity. This silent room was therefore heavily insulated to prevent sound bleeding.

The moment I saw Bride's facial expression up close, I knew what he was about to say wasn't going to be good.

"She's done in," he said, shaking his head. "I think we're on our own until New York, sir."

"What happened?"

He shrugged. "Don't know. It was working fine all through the night, and then suddenly at around three this morning it just went dead."

"Have you ever seen that happen before?"

He shook his head again. "Never. Typically, when something comes up with the system, it'll slowly start to fade... the power I mean, so the incoming and outgoing signal strength will slowly decrease for a bit before dying out. But this... it went from full power to nothing."

A moment later, Philips joined us, the same hopeless expression on his face.

"It's no use," he said. "The transmitter is completely dead. But, I don't understand it. There's no sign of a short or any kind of power surge. It's just... dead."

I understood it. I understood it very well. The past knew I was planning to intercept an important ice warning and make sure the captain saw it. Well, now it had made sure nobody would receive any message; ice warning or otherwise. *Well played,* I thought, but I wasn't about to give up.

"Do what you can with it, gentleman. Let me know if you have any luck getting it back up and running. Yeah?"

They both nodded. "Will do, sir," said Phillips.

I left the wireless room and promptly made my way to the crows nest. I needed to see if my other plan was still in place.

5

Thankfully, it was. I spoke once again to Mr. Fleet, who confirmed the binoculars were in great working order and that they'd been very helpful the past few nights. I told him (again) to look after them, and I also told him to keep a closer look out for icebergs tonight. He was concerned, but I said I just had a bad feeling about tonight and asked him to humor me. He seemed convinced enough by this explanation.

It was already after nine when I started back for my cabin. Time had a habit of flying by when you were busy (and or short on time). After the rough start to my morning, I was looking forward to getting back to Hanna. Between her mention of a headache and the paleness I saw in her face, I was worried she might have caught something. That would be the past playing an utmost cruel joke on me.

Unfortunately, I wouldn't make it.

Just as I reached the bottom of the grand staircase at C Deck, a man approached me, his expression saying this wasn't going to be a pleasant interaction. I quickly realized who he was.

"Mr. Lawson, yes?"

I nodded.

"Sir, my name is Thom—"

"Thomas King," I interrupted. "You're the Master-at-Arms."

He nodded. "Right, you seem to know everyone. He motioned back up the staircase. "Captain Smith would like to have a word. Please come with me, sir."

I was hesitant, of course, but when the Master-at-Arms requests you to follow him, you listen. This is especially true when the request is coming on behalf of the captain.

6

A moment later, although it felt much longer, I was standing in the Navigating Room, which was just off the starboard side of the Wheel House. Remember the scene from the movie *Titanic*, where Thomas Andrews meets with Captain Smith after they hit the iceberg? That's the very same room I was in now. Among me were Captain Smith, Thomas Andrews, Bruce Ismay, First Officer Murdoch, and Master-at-Arms Thomas King. I was almost certain as to why I was here, I just didn't know what was going to happen because of it.

"Ah, Mr. Lawson, thank you for joining us," said Smith, who was holding a message in his hand. "It seems you haven't been entirely honest with us, I'm afraid."

I felt a welt forming in my throat. You know, that feeling you get when you think you're going to throw up, but then nothing happens.

"I was consulted by an anonymous party who was concerned about the validity of your credentials."

Hardly anonymous, I thought. I only needed one guess as to who consulted Smith—it was Ismay, no doubt. I said none of this, of course. I'm not that stupid.

"I considered letting it go, but given the concerned party, I decided to pursue the matter further. I had Mr. Phillips send a message back to land to inquire about your prestigious appointment from Her Majesty."

And there it is. Titanic's fate is sealed—mine as well. And also, when did the wireless system start working again? Could have been the previous day, I suppose. That was most likely the case.

Smith cleared his throat. "Turns out, nobody back home has ever even heard of you, Mr. Lawson. In fact, nobody was able to find anything about anyone with that name." He paused, put the message down on the table, crossed his arms, and then stood with his eyes fixed on me. "So, tell me, who are you really?"

I sighed, more so because of what this likely meant for the ship, not so for myself. "My name really is Andrew Lawson, sir. I will swear to it."

Mr. Andrews spoke first, to Captain Smith. "I don't understand, sir. Mr. Lawson here knows this ship as well as I do. In some instances, even better, in fact. Surely an average passenger wouldn't possess such knowledge."

Smith nodded. "That is a good point, Mr. Andrews. I too had considered this."

"Oh come now," said Ismay. "He could have acquired such details from someone else on board… one of the other officers, perhaps."

That was the moment my suspicions were confirmed. Mr. Ismay was the one who talked to Captain Smith about me. *And he'll survive regardless of whether this ship sinks or not.*

Andrews shook his head. "Not all of it, Ismay. He also knows—" He paused a moment, looking between myself and the captain. "He knows about the coal fire, sir."

The tension in the room became palpable. I could already

see myself in handcuffs, locked down in one of the rooms below as Titanic steamed on into the upcoming ice field.

Captain Smith turned back to me, clearing his throat again. I don't know if it was just the situation, or perhaps the lighting, but I saw a slight paleness on his face as well. "And how did you come upon this information, Mr. Lawson? I assure you only the few in this room knew anything about such a fire."

I don't know why I said what I said next—it just came out. "I'm from the future."

The tension in the room that never really left expanded to a near unbearable level. The only sound I remember hearing was the distant splashing of the waves against the ship. If you asked me now, I'd swear a full ten minutes passed before anyone said another word.

"Do you take us for fools?" asked Ismay. "The future? Rubbish." He turned to Captain Smith. "He's a fraud, sir. I don't know what he's doing here, but I suggest you have Mr. King take him below and keep him under arrest until we reach New York."

"Rubbish?" asked Mr. Andrews. "Are you listening to what's being said, Bruce? Mr. Lawson knew about the coal fire. The men in this room are the only ones on board who knew about it… so, tell me, how did he learn of it?"

Bruce scoffed. "So, what… do you really believe that he's some time traveler from the future? I wouldn't have taken you to be so naive, Mr. Andrews."

"Not what I said at all. I'm just saying it's fairly compelling that he knows as much as he does… particularly about things there's no way he could know unless he's telling the truth."

The two of them continued to go back and forth until Smith put up his hand. "That's enough," he said, rubbing his temple and wincing. The two men went silent almost at once.

The silence lingered on for an uncomfortable amount of time until Smith finally spoke again, his gaze back on me.

"Mr. Lawson, while I agree with Mr. Andrews that your vast knowledge of this ship is hard to overlook, the idea of you being from the future is absurd." He motioned toward Mr. King. "Take him away. He's to be placed under arrest and kept locked up until we reach New York." He paused, shaking his head. "I liked you quite a lot, Mr. Lawson. I'm sorry to see you go out like this. Best of luck to you."

Mr. King took hold of my left arm and brought it behind my back. A moment later I felt the cold steel of a handcuff surrounding my wrist, followed by my right arm joining the other. He grabbed my right arm, just above my elbow, and started to lead me away. I knew I had to try one last thing—one last attempt to get someone to listen.

I momentarily broke away from him and turned around, my eyes meeting Andrews's. "She's going to sink!" His eyes, even if briefly, displayed a wave of panic. "You have to believe me! It happens tonight… an iceberg is spotted at 11:39 p.m., and a minute later she hits it. Titanic will founder!"

And then my world went dark.

7

I came to a moment later as I was being dragged down a narrow corridor, my initial guess was E Deck, but I was still pretty out of it. I was being held by two men on either side of me, and I thought I heard a third from behind. They stopped in front of a door, opened it, and brought me inside.

"Lay him down on the bed," said the third man. "I'll give

him a strong sedative that should help keep him under control."

That doesn't sound good, I remember thinking. But it was too late for me to try and fight back—I was still reeling from being knocked out.

I was more or less tossed onto the bed, which made my already painful headache infinitely worse. That was when I felt a sharp poke in my left arm, followed by a burning sensation. My vision began to become blurry almost immediately. I tried saying something about the sinking, but I couldn't understand what I was saying. The last thing I remembered from that moment was the man, who I assume was a doctor, putting away his syringe.

I remember having the most unusual dreams, mainly about random things from my life—growing up in a rural midwest town, having an early fascination with history, and eventually going to college to be a history teacher. It was like my life was flashing before my eyes, but in a series of interconnected dreams. To this day I'm not sure how to feel about such an event.

8

When I awoke again, I was lying in a small bed, one that was most uncomfortable. The room was small, not even half the size of my suite on C Deck. The next thing I noticed after the room was the whopper of a headache I still had—one of the worst I could remember. I'd find out later that Mr. King had hit me over the back of the head with a wooden mallet. Completely unnecessary if you ask me, but nobody did.

My first thought, after realizing how screwed I likely was, was wondering how long I had been out. The room I was in, which I confirmed was on E Deck, had no sign of a clock. In fact, it had nothing on the walls at all, save for a small mirror above the tiny sink next to the bed. *No first class accommodations for a supposed criminal.*

Another fun fact, although considering my circumstances, maybe not—but, I digress. The Titanic didn't actually have a "brig" of any kind. That term is related to Naval ships, not passenger ships. Remember the scene in *Titanic* where Jack is arrested and handcuffed to a pipe? Yeah, that wouldn't have happened. In fact, that room (as it was depicted on screen) didn't exist at all on the Titanic, but on her sister, the Olympic. This choice was made intentionally to give Jack a porthole to lookout, as well as a cabinet for keys.

As I stood up from the tiny bed, I looked at the equally tiny door to the cabin, wondering (hopelessly) if it was unlocked—it was not. I went to sit back down, as being vertical was causing the pounding of my head to worsen. It was then I felt the watch still in my pocket. *He didn't bother to search me.* I managed to fish it out, which was quite a task given the handcuffs, and saw it was half past six.

"Shit!"

It was all I could think of to say at the time. I'd been out for over nine hours—and time was something I had very little of.

Hanna, was my next thought. I had no way of knowing for sure, but she certainly must think I'm dead. I wondered if the captain would have any reason to apprehend her as well. I didn't think so, but it was still something that crept into my mind and wouldn't leave. *It'll be all my fault if something happens to her.* I took in a deep breath and exhaled, trying to calm myself down. If it's 6:30 now, that means there's just over five hours until the iceberg, which isn't a lot of time, especially when you're handcuffed and locked in a cabin on E Deck.

That was when a knock came at the door.

9

Thomas Andrews greeted me at the door of the tiny cabin. The first thing I noticed, which gave me much reason for concern, was the mask on his face. It forced my mind back to Hanna's headache and pale complexion—Captain Smith's, too. *Were people sick?*

I met his eyes for only a moment, then looked away, ashamed to be seen in handcuffs. He sat down next to me on the bed (there really was nowhere else to sit) and shook his head at the sight of the handcuffs.

"I'm sorry for how they've treated you," he said, pointing at the cuffs. "Those are completely unnecessary. And I did all I could to prevent the use of any sedative, but a certain few were quite insistent. I promise I'm working to get you freed."

"A sedative?" I rubbed both of my temples. My head felt like it was going to explode. "They drugged me?"

"Yes. They felt you were a risk and wanted to calm you down."

I shook my head. "I don't understand. Why are you wanting to help me then?"

He smiled, but only briefly. "Well, if I'm being honest, part of me just wants to disagree with Bruce. He can be so petty sometimes." I stifled a laugh as Andrews continued. "But, I also couldn't look past just how much you know about this ship and her crew. And lastly, I don't see you as any sort of a risk."

He stood up from the bed and paced the cabin, which

given the size wasn't much of an exercise in contemplation, if that was his goal.

"I want to believe your story, Mr. Lawson, I do. And even more than that, I want to convince the captain of it as well, however, to do that I need you to tell it to me from the beginning. Tell me everything you can."

I thought back to my conversation with Hanna, when I first told her who I really was. *Oh no, Hanna.* "Can I ask if you've heard anything about my lady, Hanna? Please tell me she isn't receiving the same treatment."

He didn't immediately respond, but his expression said plenty. *Hanna.*

"Tell me."

He sighed. "She's also being held, yes. Mr. King went for her soon after putting you in here."

"Why? She didn't have anything to do with this. Was it because she and I were involved?"

He sat back down on the bed next to me, contemplating how to tell me. "In the end, it was Bruce who ultimately convinced the captain. I don't understand why he has such a negative opinion of the two of you. In fact, he also managed to convince the captain that you two were in on a plan to sabotage the Titanic."

My mouth nearly hit the floor. "What?! On what grounds?" Even as I asked, I knew the answer. There didn't need to be any. Bruce Ismay was the chairman of the White Star Line, and his word was next to God's in the eyes of Captain Smith. Add to that my extensive knowledge of the ship, and my little outburst earlier about her doomed fate, it was no surprise that we were both in handcuffs—and drugged.

So, there I was, 107 years in the past trying to prevent the sinking of the Titanic—now accused of plotting to sink the very same ship. And to make matters worse, I got the love of my life (I know, seems fast, but the heart wants what it wants) tangled up in this mess as well. *The past fights back* played over and over in my mind.

As I looked up at Mr. Andrews, something in his eyes told me there was still more he hadn't said. *What more could there be?*

"There's more, isn't there?" I pointed to his mask, thinking back to how Hanna had looked when I last saw her. *Oh no.* "People are sick, aren't they?"

He nodded. "A lot has happened since you were brought down here. Something is happening with the passengers and crew. Over the past twenty-four hours, over 150 passengers have reported symptoms of high fever, severe head and body aches, and vomiting."

"Do you know what it is yet?"

"It wasn't immediately apparent, no. With the symptoms mentioned, it could just be a bad cold, or maybe the flu, however, this afternoon several passengers began showing a rash on their face."

Uh oh, I thought. *I knew my history well enough to know what fever, body aches, vomiting, and a rash amounted to.*

"Our doctor onboard, Dr O'Loughlin, is now thinking it's smallpox, hence the masks. I've brought you one, although despite your extensive interactions while on board, you seem fine."

Even more proof of my story about being from the future.

Thanks to James's foresight, he had vaccinated me for just about every disease known to man, including smallpox. *Thank you, James.* This, however, didn't mean I couldn't still transmit the awful disease.

"In 2019, where I'm from, we've completely irradiated

smallpox from the world. I also received a vaccination for it just before my trip back here in case an outbreak occurred. Sounds like that was a good idea after all." I tried to smile.

Andrews nodded in agreement. "Yes, a good idea indeed. A select few of us onboard, myself included, have also received a vaccine, although, I imagine it isn't nearly as effective as the one from your time. And as I'm sure you know, we're still able to transmit the disease." He handed me the mask. "Better to be safer than sorry."

My thoughts went to Hanna. *Could I have given her smallpox?* The mere idea made me shudder. I couldn't live with myself if that were true.

I took the mask and fumbled it on, which was made more difficult with handcuffs. "Is the outbreak serious?" I knew it was even before I asked. While I couldn't deny our healthcare system of today needs plenty of work, the state of medical care in 1912 was abysmal at best. Mr. Andrews confirmed what I had been thinking.

"It is, I'm afraid. Our doctor and his assistance have quarantined the most serious of cases as best they can, but there's only so much that can be done while at sea. Unfortunately, we don't have much for medical supplies on board outside of the basics."

My head was spinning with the news of this outbreak. *Was this the past continuing to fight me?* Deep down, I knew it was.

"Does the captain know?"

He nodded, a darkness coming over him. "More so than he'd like, I'm afraid. He has been quarantined to his quarters after sores appeared on his face. Several of the officers have also reported these symptoms. We could have a pretty serious outbreak on our hands."

"How can I help?" I didn't really know what else to say,

given the situation. I was handcuffed in a cabin on E Deck, after all.

"Will you tell me your story?" asked Andrews. "I want to help you, and if what you said earlier is true, we don't have much time. The smallpox situation is very unfortunate timing, but perhaps it's a moot point if she's really going to sink."

It dawned on me then that perhaps the real reason Titanic sank was due to this smallpox outbreak. I had never read a single article mentioning such an outbreak, but when something happened over 100 years ago (during a time when the printed word was the most common way of receiving information), it's understandable (and almost assumed) that certain facts would be lost.

"If you're willing to listen, I'll tell you everything."

He sat down on the bed next to me. "If there's a chance you can save my ship, you have my complete attention."

And with that, I told him everything.

10

I started with who I really was. I told him about teaching history in a small town in 2019, and that my extensive knowledge of Titanic came from my fascination with the ship and the tragedy surrounding her. It must have struck him as odd to hear the very ship we were presently on board referred to in the past tense—but then again, everything about this situation was odd.

When I got to the part about James and his time travel device, the Anode Reactor, he had questions. Who wouldn't?

"How does such a device operate? Surely the power you'd need for something like that is immense… almost impossibly so."

"Remember, I'm just a history teacher, so I don't know all of the details, but I remember James saying something about a breakthrough chemical reaction along with a highly resistant material capable of harnessing the resulting power."

He was in awe. "Incredible. Please, continue."

If that wasn't enough for a man in 1912, the next bit would really do him in. I told him about James discovering a parallel universe in which the Titanic never sank, and because of this, one of her passengers went on to eradicate disease as we know it. The flu, pneumonia, aids (not that Andrews knew what that was), and even cancer. Andrews was a smart man, of this I know for sure, but he couldn't fathom such a thing. But again, who could?

He was too absorbed in this idea to ask any questions, so I continued with my story. I told him my initial plan was to try and get close to the crew and convince them of what was to become of the ship but quickly realized this idea would never work.

He nodded. "Because of their blindness caused by arrogance and naivety."

I was taken aback by this response. I agreed, of course, but to actually hear it from him was surprising. I think he saw this on my face.

"I know what you're thinking," he said. "But, while I may be among the payroll of White Star, I disagree with many of their decisions as of late, particularly around these new Olympic liners."

I considered diving deeper into that, but thought better of it a moment later. There was no time. Instead, I continued on with my story, telling him that I provided the lookouts with a pair of binoculars. He was surprised to hear that they didn't have them. I also told him I'd asked both wireless operators to inform me of each and every ice warning they receive today—there would be five in total.

"How does she sink?" he asked. It was one of the few questions he had asked the entire time. "Her watertight compartments should have kept her afloat, even if four were compromised."

It didn't escape me that he was now using the past tense—he believed me that she was going to sink if nothing was done. I thought that would have given me a sense of relief, but it somehow didn't.

"That's right", I said. "Unfortunately, just the right circumstances aligned that night… Well, tonight. When she hits, she scrapes along her starboard side for nearly 300 feet, punching holes in the hull and compromising five compartments."

His expression was filled with horror. "Five compartments? Christ, what luck that is."

"It gets worse, I'm afraid. Thanks to the runaway coal fire, the bulkhead in between those two coal bunkers is thought to have been weakened. I say it that way because there's still controversy to this day surrounding the fire. Regardless, that bunker eventually gives out and a sixth compartment is compromised, rapidly increasing her sinking."

He stood up again and paced, shaking his head back and forth as he did so. I saw him stop and look at his watch.

"6:48," he said. "Can you lay out the timeline for me?"

If ever there was someone who could, it was me. The timeline of that night, tonight, was deeply ingrained in my memory. I had studied it for countless hours, sometimes days at a time.

"I can.

"The iceberg is spotted at 11:39 p.m.

"A minute later, Titanic hits it and begins taking on water.

"At midnight, you will have assessed the damage and inform the captain that she will founder.

"12:17 a.m., the Carpathia picks up Titanic's distress signal and proceeds to steam towards her. Unfortunately, she won't make it in time.

"12:25 a.m., the first lifeboat, lifeboat 7, is lowered into the water with only twenty-eight people

"2:05 a.m., the water reaches the Boat Deck.

"2:18 a.m., Titanic breaks in two, just aft of her third funnel.

"2:20 a.m., she sinks."

I let out a heavy sigh as I look at Mr. Andrews, who has stopped pacing, and is staring blankly at the adjacent wall. Not surprising, it's a lot to take in.

"I—I know it's a lot, and there's more than will happen, but what I laid out are the key events."

He nodded and cleared his throat. "It's a terribly weird sensation, this conversation we're having right now, Mr. Lawson. You speak with such… such confidence and conviction, I don't see how it could be possible for you to be making any of this up. I believe your story, Andrew."

It felt absolutely amazing to hear him say he believed me. I knew we were far from out of the water (an awful pun, but I said it), but it was a start.

"Thank you," I said. "That means a lot. But will the captain believe it? Or, Mr. Ismay?"

He considered this, sitting down on the bed with me again. "I don't know. If I were you, I wouldn't count on it. I think you'll be on your own."

I motioned around the room, which was made awkward

by the handcuffs. "On my own to do what? I'm still under arrest, remember?"

He smiled and pulled a key from his jacket pocket. "I really shouldn't be doing this, but to hell with it. I believe what you say to be true, and I told you I'd help if I could." He removed my handcuffs, to which my wrists were most grateful.

"I don't know how to thank you," I said. "I—"

Another knock came at the door.

11

Mr. Andrews got up and answered the door. It was my steward, Smethells. *What in the world is he doing down here?* Andrews stepped outside, and I heard their hushed voices discussing something—it sounded serious. I heard a loud sigh come from Mr. Andrews as he thanked the steward and closed the cabin door.

"What was my steward doing down here?"

I didn't like what I saw in his eyes as he responded. "Remember the sickness I told you about earlier?"

I did, and it didn't take me but a fraction of a second to realize what he was about to tell me. *Please be wrong.*

"Smethells has been discreetly checking in on your lady, and well—" He stopped, cleared his throat again. "She's developed the same symptoms as many of the others, including a severe rash on her face. Her fever is over 104, Mr. Lawson. Apparently it's been that way for several hours. To make matters worse, she hasn't been able to keep anything down, not even water, so dehydration is a major concern."

I felt my heart rate increase as I tried to take in what he was saying. *Hanna is sick, critically so by the sounds of it. And worst of all, I most likely gave it to her.* I knew then that while the

Titanic was approaching her fate, I needed to go to Hanna first.

I stood up, now face to face with Mr. Andrews. "I need to see her. Where is she being held? Can I get to her?"

He sighed. "She was put in cabin E-17, and not unintentionally, we're in E-98."

"Ugh, of course." Those two cabins couldn't be much farther apart. An idea came to me then. "Mr. Andrews, perhaps this smallpox outbreak could work to our advantage. I imagine with both passengers and crew affected, the two of us are much less of a priority."

I saw a smirk form on his face. "I always knew you were a smart man, Mr. Lawson. He put out his hand to shake mine. "Like I said, I believe you, Andrew. I'm grateful for all the effort you've put in to saving this ship, more than I could ever express in words, but I hope what I've done here this evening is at least a start. Go do whatever it is you have to. If you need anything else from me, I'll likely be in the smoking room." He handed me the handcuff key. "This will also work for Hanna's restraints. Best of luck, Mr. Lawson."

I proudly shook his hand. "Thank you very much, Mr. Andrews. I will do everything I can to save Titanic, I promise."

A moment later I left cabin E-98, still feeling a bit drowsy from the sedative, but the conversation with Mr. Andrews had brought some clarity back to my mind. I peeked at my pocket watch—7:25 p.m.

I needed to get to Hanna.

CHAPTER XI

FOUR HOURS UNTIL DISASTER

1

I raced towards the bow end of E Deck. I was once again thankful for my extensive knowledge of the Titanic. It certainly made situations like this one easier. As I approached E-17, I saw Smethells was standing outside the cabin, who was also wearing a mask. He seemed happy to see me.

"Ah, Mr. Lawson. I'm sorry to have been the bearer of such bad news. I was only following orders, sir."

I nodded my understanding. "I know, Smethells. Thank you. I need to see her."

He bowed slightly and motioned towards the door. "If asked, I saw nothing."

"Thank you," I said, slowly opening the door and closing it behind me.

Hanna and I locked eyes. She was sitting up in the bed, her handcuffed wrists folded in her lap, and I could see the sores forming on her face from the awful disease that was now attacking her body. Despite how terrible she must have felt, her face lit up when she saw me

"Oh, Andrew! You came for me!" She tried to get up, but grimaced as the pain surging through her body was too much. "Ahh, sorry. I—I can't really move too much right now."

It pained me to see her like she was. It was also scary to see just how fast she had declined over the past nine or so hours. I walked over and carefully sat down on the bed beside her, wrapping an arm around her.

"I'm so sorry for what's happened." I went in to kiss her cheek but she pulled away.

"I—I don't want you to get this. It's terribly painful."

I shook my head. "I'm vaccinated for it… I won't get it." I couldn't bear to tell her I was likely the one who gave it to her… not yet, anyway. I gave her a kiss on the cheek and hugged her tightly. She let out a heavy sigh as she did her best to hold me while handcuffed.

"These wretched things are the worst," she said, holding out her hands.

"Oh, right." I took out the key from my jacket. "We have at least one believer on board." I gently grabbed the handcuffs, one by one, and unlocked them. "There."

She rubbed her wrists, clearly thankful to not have them cuffed. "Oh, thank you so much. It's so good to see you again. When they took me I—I didn't know what to think." She threw her arms around me properly and we hugged one another. It was a reunion I knew I wouldn't soon forget—if ever. Unfortunately, there was much still to be done.

I pulled away and met her gaze. I saw pain in her eyes, but I knew it was mostly from the disease.

"How much have you heard about the outbreak?"

"Not much," she said, leaning back against the bed's metal

headboard. "Just that the doctor thinks it's smallpox. I don't really know much about it, though."

I tried to hide my concern, but between how much I cared for her and my lack of any kind of poker face, it was quite apparent.

"But you do, don't you?" she asked. "How bad? Please don't lie to me."

I sighed. "It's smallpox. I'm 99.9% certain of that. And it's very serious, I'm afraid. In a day or two, you'll start to feel better, but that's a false hope. A couple days later your fever will return with a vengeance as the rash spreads over most of your body." I stopped, unsure of how far to go.

She took in a deep breath and let it out, a little shaky from the sound of it. "I'm going to die from this, aren't I?" The question caught me off guard, but I kept it together, given the circumstances. I wanted to make something up, but she read my mind. "Please, just tell me, Andrew. I can already see it in your face."

I nodded. "Without proper medical attention, more than can be given in the middle of the Atlantic, most likely." At that moment I made up my mind. I took her hand in mine. "But I'm not going to let that happen. I'm taking you back to 2019 with me and we'll get you the best medical care available. You'll be fine, I promise."

Yes, I knew what I was saying. I was giving up on the Titanic to save Hanna. Because the act of using the Anode Reactor had such a negative impact on the human body, this would be the last trip I could take. And I was more than willing to do this to save the woman I wanted to spend the rest of my life with. The past was already winning this fight anyway.

Hanna shook her head adamantly. She took my hand in

both of hers and locked eyes with me. "Andrew, I need you to listen to me very carefully. Okay?" I nodded, knowing all too well what was about to happen. "I won't let you sacrifice your mission because of me. I won't." I wanted to speak, but she put up a hand. "No, I won't hear of it. This ship is too important to you… it's been your life's study!"

"Hanna, I can't do th—"

She put her hand up to my cheek. "You can do this. You're likely the only one on Earth who can." She sighed. "Don't get me wrong, it hurts like hell to say this, but in my heart I know it's the right thing to do. If I let you save me, I know I'd never be able to forgive myself. Think of all the people that will be saved… and not just from the ship not sinking. You said the alternative universe or whatever was rid of all disease, right?"

"Yes, Hanna, but that's not guaranteed. Sure, it happened that way in that alternative universe, but we can't know for sure if it'll play out the same way in ours. Even if I save the Titanic, and Cillian makes it to New York as intended, the butterfly effect can still impact the timeline at any point."

Without missing a beat she had a response ready. "But there is a chance." Reluctantly, I nodded. "And if you choose to save me instead, there's none. The choice is obvious, my dear. I need you to do this for me. Andrew, I love you very much, and I'm incredibly grateful for all you've done for me in the short time we've known one another. I'll never forget it."

I wanted more than anything to continue this argument, but time was quickly running out. If I waited any longer, I wouldn't be able to save Hanna or the Titanic. So, despite my heart telling me not to, I gave in and agreed with her.

"Okay, okay. If that's how it's going to be, I best get to

work. There's less than four hours until Titanic has her date with the iceberg."

"What's your plan? Check with the lookouts?"

I hadn't really figured out my next move, but that was as good of one as any. "Yeah, I think that's a good idea. I better get myself up to the crow's nest." I leaned in and kissed her, careful to avoid the rash. "Will you be okay?"

She nodded, her eyes showing her sadness. "Don't worry about me, just worry about saving the ship. Be careful, Andrew."

With that, I left the cabin, said farewell to Smethells, and made my way (slowly but surely) up to the Forecastle Deck.

2

To my surprise, I had no trouble making it up top from E Deck. I passed only one officer, who was helping a few other sick passengers back to their quarters. He met my glance, and even with his mask I saw it was fourth officer Boxhall, but he must not have registered who I was. Or, maybe he didn't actually know who I was. I tried to think back to whether or not we'd met but couldn't do it. Aside from this interaction, I saw a handful of other passengers wandering the ship, all of whom appeared to be restless and worried.

I stopped in front of the ladder leading up the crow's nest. I listened closely and heard hushed voices from above. In the past I had gotten lucky lining up my visits with Mr. Fleet being on duty, however, I knew he would be on duty this evening. He was, after all, the one who first spotted the infamous iceberg.

"Mr. Fleet?" I called up. "Got a moment?"

There was a moment of silence, which caused another spike in my anxiety. *What if they'd been told to keep an eye out for me? I might have just sealed my fate—and Hanna's—and Titanic's.* Thankfully, my anxiety proved to be for not.

"Mr. Lawson? That you?" I said it was. "Be right down." I heard him climb down the ladder, one step at a time, until he got to me. "Good evening, sir. Brr, sure is a cold one ain't it?"

"It is. Cold and calm," I agreed. "Still got those binoculars?"

"Sure do," he said proudly. "They've been a lifesaver for the eyes. Say, I heard some not so pleasant news 'bout you earlier today. Someone was saying you were some spy sent onboard to sabotage the ship. Bunch of rubbish if you ask me."

I had started to get worried until that last sentence. "You don't believe the rumors?"

He scoffed. "Heck no, Mr. Lawson. From what I've seen, you've got a fascination with this ship rivaled only by Mr. Andrews. The way I see it, you'd never do anything to endanger Titanic."

I let out a sigh of relief. "Thank you, Fleet. I appreciate it. I—"

Just as I was about to remind him of the importance of those binoculars, a crash on the deck below the crow's nest caught our attention. We ran to the front of the Forecastle Deck, and my heart sank as we saw the broken binoculars lying on the deck. *The past scores again.* We looked up to the crow's nest, where Reginald Lee had both his hands up on his head, clearly ashamed at being so careless.

I sighed. "So much for that."

Fleet picked up the binoculars and shook his head. "Sure am sorry about this, Mr. Lawson. I should have taken them down here with me."

"Not your fault," I said, putting my hand on his shoulder.

"Anyway, you better get back up top. Keep a sharp lookout... the sea will be like glass with as calm as it is tonight." He bid me farewell and made his way back to the crow's nest.

As I stood on the Forecastle Deck, holding the pair of now useless binoculars, I realized the past was, for lack of a better phrase, kicking my butt.

3

Trust me, at that moment I really considered just throwing in the towel and heading back to 2019 with Hanna. With just over three hours to go until disaster, both of my plans had been ruined by the past fighting back. Not to mention the fact I was supposed to be under arrest for supposedly trying to sabotage Titanic. And to top things off, a smallpox outbreak was causing quite a panic among the passengers (and some of the crew, too).

While I was allowing myself this brief pity party, my mind went back to 2019—back to my classroom, teaching seniors about the pivotal moments in history. Until one day an old man shows up claiming to have invented time travel and asks me to save the Titanic from sinking. It seemed like so long ago that I had met him outside the school to go see his lab, and he dropped another bombshell on me—saying he's also able to telepo—*wait a minute,* I thought, interrupting myself. *Teleportation... James's Anode Reactor can also teleport things. Could that be the solution?*

Without a moment to waste, I sprinted from the Forecastle deck, leaving the broken binoculars behind, and headed for my cabin. I didn't know for sure if they'd left my stuff alone when I was arrested, but I was counting on the smallpox outbreak to be enough to keep them busy. Again, on my way through the decks I saw a few people in passing, but for the most part the passengers had turned in early—due to either being quarantined or the bone chilling weather Titanic was currently sailing through.

I stopped in front of my cabin and realized I didn't have a key anymore. *Had I given Hanna a key?* I didn't think so. What would be the use? She was with me nearly all the time. Thinking my luck might change, I reached for the handle and tried it. To my surprise, it turned and then I was standing in my cabin—with what looked to be all of my stuff, undisturbed. *Perhaps it was my turn for some good luck.*

After digging through both of my suitcases, I finally found the minuscule communications device, i.e., a high-tech earpiece that James had sent with me. He was quite insistent on making sure I hid it well to avoid someone else finding it. I'd say I did well—I barely found it myself. I should probably further clarify *miniscule.* The entirety of the device is about the size of a kernel of corn—crazy small for such an advanced piece of technology. *Let's just hope I can get it to function.*

4

Thankfully (and not surprisingly), the moment I put the thing in my ear I heard a bright chime, along with a greeting from whom I assumed to be that AI running James's lab. The voice sounded familiar, anyway.

"Hello," said the voice. "Please state your full name for vocal recognition."

I cleared my throat, a bit nervous as I wasn't expecting a test. "Andrew Lawson."

A moment later, "Vocal analysis confirmed. Good evening,

Andrew. Please confirm the initiation of space-time sequencing."

I assumed that was what would connect me to James. "I confirm."

"Thank you. Initiating sequencing now. Time to connect… ten seconds."

Precisely ten seconds later, I heard a *click* and then another voice.

"Andrew, is that you?" asked James. "Everything okay?"

"James! Man, am I glad to hear your voice. I can't believe these tiny earpieces are allowing us to communicate. How wild."

He laughed—that type of laugh only an old man can have, which was followed by a coughing fit. His health was getting quite poor, unfortunately. It made me wonder just how many times he had used the device, and how many different timelines he'd visited. I'd have to ask him sometime if I ever got the chance.

"I hope you didn't call just to test out the connection," he said. "The amount of energy we're using to talk right now would blow your mind."

An understatement, I'm sure. "I have no doubt about that, James. But no, I did have something I needed to talk to you about, and I don't have much time."

"That was another reason I was surprised to hear from you… figured you'd be awfully busy right about now. Only a couple hours until your deadline. Anyway, what can I do for you? Always willing to help if I can."

I sure hope you can, I thought.

"Well," I said. "I'm kind of screwed at the moment, if I'm being completely honest." I found myself pacing around my cabin while picking at my nails. I didn't want to admit I'd failed, but I kinda had. "The two plans I had fell through… like you said, the past has been fighting me pretty hard. On top of that, there's a smallpox outbreak onboard, which I hadn't heard of such a thing happening, but maybe that's just the butterfly effect."

James whistled. "Sounds like a bit of a mess back there. What exactly are you needing my help with? I'm sorry, but I can't risk using the Anode Reactor again myself… I just don't think my body can take it."

The sadness in his voice was evident, even across a wormhole through space and time. The man just wanted to do all he could to help everyone. I had a huge level of respect for him, one that would continue to grow for the rest of our lives.

"No, nothing like that," I said. "I, uhh… I was thinking about the Reactor's teleportation ability. Is there any chance something like that could be done to teleport the Titanic out of the massive ice field she's about to plow into?"

The silence that fell over the call lasted so long I thought the connection dropped, which wouldn't have surprised me. We were literally talking through a wormhole, spanning 107 years. I was about to ask if he was still there when I heard him clear his throat.

"Yo—you want to teleport the Titanic?"

There was something odd in his voice when he asked the question. *Was it fear?* I didn't know James well enough to be sure, but it sounded an awful like fear in his question.

I sighed. "I know, it's probably not even possible. I just.. I don't know what to do, James. I'm left with an impossible decision." I stopped for a moment to compose myself. I didn't want to cry. "I didn't tell you right away, but Hanna has contracted smallpox, and she's declining rapidly. If something isn't done soon…"

"And if you bring her back here, you lose Titanic."

"Well, you said using the device more would cause irreparable damage to my body. Although, I'm thinking at this point I'd be willing to risk that if it meant I could save both Hanna and Titanic."

"What I said was partially true. I don't know for sure if one additional trip would cause irreparable damage, however, what I do know is that when I sent you back to 1912, it was the farthest I'd ever used the Anode Reactor for. It's caused some… complications in keeping the wormhole open between the two timelines."

"Listen, James… I unfortunately don't have time to ask about the complications, and frankly, I doubt I'd understand of word of it anyway. The situation here is quickly becoming dire. Is there any chance this can be done? To teleport Titanic out of the ice field."

"You're asking about teleporting the Titanic… a ship weighing what, 55,000 tons?" She weighed 52,310 tons, but I didn't say anything. I knew what he was getting at. "Not to mention the teleportation would have to be initiated remotely through the wormhole."

I wasn't sure how to respond. "So…"

He sighed. "Look, there was this one time.."

Jesus, has he teleported something this size before? How would that not have been reported on? And how would I have not heard of something like that? Being a history teacher and all, surely it would have been a key event in maritime history.

"I know what you're thinking," he said, as if reading my mind. "It was codenamed the Philadelphia Experiment. And you haven't heard of it because it was declared top secret by the CIA, after the urging of the US Navy… and, after what happened to the crew."

My mind was racing. Even though time was something I had little of, I was dying to know more. "What are you talking about?"

"It was a long time ago, 1943 I believe. I had traveled back to that year at random, wanting to test out the capabilities of my newly discovered teleportation technology. I figured back then there were less people to become witnesses. Anyway, I picked a Navy vessel as a test subject, the USS Eldridge. It wasn't huge, but it was significantly larger than anything else I'd tested with. It was docked at a remote location, and it was late at night… I thought it was empty. If I had known…"

His voice trailed off. So many thoughts ran through my mind. What was James saying? I needed to get him talking again.

"Wh—what happened? Did the test not work?"

"Well, yes and no. I was able to successfully teleport the ship. Unfortunately, when I brought it back, well… the crew had not returned in the proper state of matter." There was a brief pause. "Andrew, they came back embedded into the structure of the ship. I unintentionally murdered a crew of nearly one hundred men."

"Holy shit." Not subtle, I know, but it was all I could say. No wonder the mention of teleporting Titanic put him on edge. I can't imagine the trauma something like that must leave. "Sorry, that wasn't very nice of me to say. That must have been… I don't even know how someone would react to that."

Another sigh from him. "It took me a very long time to move past it. But, I can't let that get in the way of me helping you. After all, I'm the reason you're back there in the first place."

I was taken aback. "What? No, James, I couldn't ask you

to help now. I—I'll figure something out." This was a blatant lie. I was screwed if James couldn't help. "Besides, wouldn't we just end up like the people on the Eldridge did?"

I heard what sounded like furious typing on a keyboard before he responded. "I know what went wrong in 1943. It wasn't that the device couldn't teleport something of that size, it just didn't have the precise dimensional points for reference to properly return the crew to their previous positions. It got a 'rough estimation' of them, which would be less troublesome for inanimate objects, but not so much with humans."

Despite the predicament I was in, and thinking I was a fairly smart guy in general, I just couldn't wrap my tiny history brain around what he was saying.

"Could I have that in a version a lowly history teacher might understand? Are you saying you think you could actually teleport the Titanic without harming anyone onboard?"

I heard a few more keystrokes. "Yes, I think so. I need to run a few calculations first." I couldn't begin to imagine what kind of Einstein levels of math he was about to perform. "How much does Titanic weigh?"

An answer I know! "52,310 tons."

More typing. "Length?"

"882 ft, 9in."

And more typing. "Width?"

Oh, that one I had to dig for. "92 ft. 6in."

A bit more typing followed, and then I heard what sounded like hands clapping today. "Bingo," he said. "I think it can be done." I couldn't help but sense a 'but' coming.

"What's the catch?"

"There's a few," he said, more furious typing ensuing. "Do you have the platform handy?"

I went back into my suitcases and found the coaster

looking device. *I'm still surprised none of the officers took any of my stuff.*

"Got it. Do you want me to activate it?"

"I've got it."

Before I could ask, the device began instructing me to set it down on a level surface, just as it had when Hanna and I used it. I followed its instructions, carefully putting it onto the floor.

"Thanks for the warning. What are you doing by the way? Am I coming to your lab?"

"Nope, I'm sending you three triangulation devices. I'm uh, going to need you to place them at precise locations throughout the ship. Can you do that?"

I almost said yes right away, but then I wondered—*could I do that?* Prior to the whole getting arrested thing, it wouldn't have been a problem—but now? I'd have to be extra careful. I glanced at my watch, which was ticking away, and noted it was 8:30. *And I need to be extra quick.*

"It could get tricky, but I don't think I really have a choice." I sighed. "I'll make it happen."

"Good. Without these devices in place, I can't guarantee any part of this plan will work."

"Understood."

"Okay, just a few more things to input here, and we're ready. Initializing the AR to send the devices. Sending in 3, 2, 1."

The platform began to emit a high pitched noise as it began to vibrate. A moment later, both of these stopped and were followed by a bright flash of light. When I looked again, I saw what I assumed were the three triangulation devices resting on the platform. I slowly approached, carefully picking one of them up. They looked like small metal disks, a little smaller than a CD.

"All three are here," I said. "How do these work? Anything I should know?"

"They're pretty straightforward. The important thing is they need to be placed as precisely to the coordinates as possible. I'm sending you those now, along with a blueprint of the ship showing those coordinates."

I quickly moved the other two devices off the platform, just in time for a large stack of printouts to take their place. I picked them up, and saw that they were full scale prints of all the decks of Titanic—the detail was astounding.

"Do you just have this stuff lying around? How did you get these so quickly?"

James laughed. And then coughed. I liked the former, not so much the latter.

"I told you, I like being prepared. Anyway, I marked the exact locations you'll need to place them. I imagine the most difficult will be the one down in the engine room."

I agreed. That would be a bit of a pain, but it's not like I had any other option. I looked for the other two points—one was on A Deck, on the starboard side of the First Class Smoking Room. The last one, not too surprisingly, was right at the tip of the bow. I figured I'd save that one for last. I took another look at my watch—*gah, nine p.m. is quickly approaching.*

"I better get on this, James. There isn't much time left."

"Agreed. Listen, Andrew… there's one more thing."

There always is, I thought. I didn't have a great feeling about what was coming.

"Let's have it then, James."

He sighed. "Andrew, the amount of energy we're talking about to pull this off…"

I didn't like the pause—not one bit. "Just how much

energy are we talking about? Would I even be able to comprehend it?"

"Remember the detonation of Tsar Bomba by the Soviets?"

"Of course. It was the largest nuclear detonation in history."

"Right. Well, the output of that was about 210 petajoules. If my math is correct, and it usually is, to pull this off we'll be looking at generating close to 5 million zettajoules."

I didn't know how to respond to that. I knew what a joule was, but not those other things he was talking about.

"I—I don't know what those are, James. What's a zettajoule?"

"Think of it this way… the entire world population consumes about half a zettajoule annually, give or take."

Now that was something I could understand. *Jesus, this is unreal. How did I get myself into this?*

"How?" I asked. "How are you possibly going to generate that kind of energy?"

"That's why I brought it up. In order to do it, I'll need to overload the Anode Reactor. Usually it has a failsafe to avoid a runaway reaction, but in this case I have no alternative but to bypass it."

"Won't that be dangerous?"

"Yes, but a lot of that energy will be dispersed through the wormhole. Unfortunately, the reactor won't be able to withstand the remaining energy from the runaway reaction. Once I initialize the teleport, there's no turning back. Do you understand what I'm saying?"

I did. Somehow I knew from the moment he said there was one more thing. If I have James teleport Titanic out of harm's way, I'll be stuck in 1912 forever.

"I read you, James. It could be worse though, right? If this works, I'll be able to see Titanic complete her maiden voyage."

There was a moment of silence on James's end. "You're a good man, Andrew. Your dedication to that ship is honorable. But look, you best get going and place those devices. I'll do the remaining calculations needed on my end in the meantime. I don't want to risk the energy consumption by leaving this connection active, but take your earpiece with you, and reach out if something comes up. Okay?"

"Understood. Thank you for your help, James. Talk soon."

I heard the connection end, and then silence fell over my cabin. I had a mammoth undertaking to do, and less than three hours to do it in. It was now or never.

I stuffed the triangulation devices into my suit, put my hat and mask on, and left my cabin for the engine room.

CHAPTER XII

TWO HOURS UNTIL DISASTER

1

As I left my cabin, the thought crossed my mind to go check on Hanna, especially since it would essentially be on the way. Ultimately, I chose against it due to the limited amount of time I had. Because if I failed to install these triangulation devices, Titanic would hit the iceberg as history has said it did for over 100 years, and none of what Hanna and I have shared would matter. I'd likely die from hypothermia from the frigid waters of the North Atlantic, and Hanna would either suffer the same fate, or a combination of that and Smallpox. I did my best to push those thoughts out of my head.

I made my way down the second class staircase, which was the easiest way to get down to the engine room from where I had been on C Deck. The first spot James marked on the blueprints was inside Boiler Room 3, which was on Titanic's Tank Top Deck—the bottom-most deck of the ship. I made my way to the Orlop Deck, which was just above the Tank

Top, to try and get a better vantage point to my target. I didn't know how far the word of my arrest had spread, but I couldn't afford to take any chances.

The Orlop Deck had several access ports in the floor by which the boiler rooms below could be accessed. I quietly opened one of these and looked down into Boiler Room 3—the heat and smoke from the burning coal hit me with tremendous force. I had to fight back a coughing fit, although with the level of noise being what it was down there, it's unlikely I'd have been heard. I decided to take a risk and act as if my arrest didn't happen. I had remembered my master engineer badge, which was around my neck as I climbed the ladder down into the boiler room.

2

Down in Boiler Room 3, the first person to acknowledge me was one of the trimmers. I touched on them a bit already, but trimmers really did have the worst job of anyone else onboard—and the worst pay. Their job was to keep the distribution of a ship's coal even throughout the bunkers. This involved moving coal between the bunkers, as well as making sure the stokers had adequate coal to feed into the hungry boilers of Titanic. It was back-breaking work, for abysmal pay, but it was a vital role to keeping the ship 'trim' or level in the water.

"Good evening, sir," the trimmer said, greeting me with a respectful nod and stopping with his wheelbarrow. "Something I can do for you?"

It was clear this man had no knowledge of what happened on the Boat Deck. For many of the men down here, that area of the ship was another world. I told him that I was just having a look around before turning in for the night. A lie, I know, but desperate times and all that. The trimmer nodded again and bid me farewell as he grunted and pushed along his wheelbarrow full of coal.

The spot on the blueprints was located on the port side wall in Boiler Room 3, right next to Coal Bunker J. I made my way through the cramped pathway towards the wall—the coal bunker on my left and the boilers, stokers, and firemen on my right. A few gave me confused looks, likely due to seeing a suit down here, but for the most part they were indifferent towards my presence—perfect.

A moment later I was standing next to the port side wall of the boiler room. I did my best not to look suspicious, although given the circumstances, this wasn't particularly easy. That being said, I was thankful for the size of the devices James gave me—they were easily hidden inside my suit pocket. I took one last look around, and seeing that no one was paying me much mind, I slipped one of the devices onto the wall, just behind the last boiler.

I turned back the way I came and headed toward the ladder leading upward. I had both hands and one foot on the first step when I heard a voice call out to me.

"Mr. Lawson?" My heart sank at first, but then I thought I knew the voice. I turned around to see a sweaty, dirty faced Fred Barrett leaning against an iron rod used for stoking the boilers. "It is you. Sure didn't think I'd be seeing you again."

I managed to let go of the ladder and approach Fred, still keeping myself on edge. "He—hello, Mr. Barret. I was just having another look around."

I couldn't read his expression, but something about his body language told me he wasn't about to try and apprehend me. I wasn't great at reading people, so I could have been dead wrong.

He motioned up the ladder with his head. "I'll follow you up."

Begrudgingly, I turned back around and went up the ladder to the Orlop Deck. A moment later, Fred followed and closed the hatch. My heart felt like it was in my throat.

"I'll cut to it, Mr. Lawson, as I don't think you have much time." He looked around, making sure nobody was around. This wasn't an issue as this part of the deck was mostly unoccupied. "I heard from some officers up top about you being arrested."

Shit. But, maybe he doesn't believe their lies about me. "Look, Mr. Barrett—"

He held up a hand. "Don't worry, Mr. Lawson, I'm not about to take you to them or anything like that. After this conversation, if asked, I'll say I haven't seen you."

I felt an enormous amount of stress fall from my body. "Oh, thank god," I said. "It's been a rough last few hours, Mr. Barrett. But, why are you covering for me?"

"Just a feeling, I guess. Officer Murdoch told me everything that happened, and while I don't know how to feel about the time traveling part of your story, I sure as hell don't buy their rubbish version where you're here to sabotage the ship."

I was beside myself. *Another ally,* I thought. "What makes you think that? You barely know me."

He smiled. "Fleet and I are good mates. We've discussed you a fair bit when our breaks line up. He says you're a good man, and if he says so, that's good enough for me."

He paused—I could tell he wanted to ask about something, and I was almost certain I knew what it was, especially if he'd heard everything from Murdoch.

I was right.

"I gotta ask," he began again. "Is she really going to sink?"

I pulled out my watch and saw it was fast approaching ten —*ugh, I really have to pick things up.* I nodded to Barrett. "In just under two hours, Fleet will spot a massive iceberg in the dark and calm waters. Unfortunately, it will already be too late by the time Murdoch orders the wheel hard to starboard. A little over two and a half hours later, she'll dip under the water in two pieces, taking 1,500 lives down with her."

He stood silently, staring at me to see if my expression faltered. His changed to something like understanding once he saw I was serious. Barrett was a strong man, one of the good ones, and I knew he'd fight until his last breath to look after the men he supervised down below. But, I also knew that if I stayed here with him much longer, it wouldn't matter.

"Look, I gotta get going. I'm going to prevent this. Titanic won't sink on my watch." I put out my hand. "I appreciate what you're doing, Barrett. You're a good man."

He shook my hand, a rare smile forming on his face. "You as well, Mr. Lawson. Good luck with whatever it is you're doing to save her. If I can help, you know where to find me."

I nodded to him again and made haste out of there, making my way upward toward A Deck. It would be the last time I saw Frederick Barrett.

3

Before continuing upward, I initiated the device in my ear and was greeted again by the voice of Anasi. After verifying who I was, the connection across time and space was made.

"Hello? James?" I said. "You there?"

"I'm here, Andrew. How are things going?"

It still blew my mind that I was talking to him from 107 years in the past. I don't know if that's something I'll ever be able to accept, despite having lived through it.

"I just placed the first device with no issues. I've made my share of enemies onboard, but thankfully I still have some allies as well."

I heard a bit of typing from his side. "Very good. I'm still working out some of the numbers here. I'm sure you can imagine it's not exactly high school math I'm doing."

An understatement if I'd ever heard one. "I actually can't imagine, James, but I'll take your word for it. Can we still do this?"

There was a silence that didn't comfort me. "Yes, but it's going to be tight. You need to get the other two devices installed quickly. I still need to calibrate them, and I can't do that until all three are installed and operational."

"How long will that take?"

More typing. "About five minutes, give or take. It's hard to know for sure as all of this is happening through a wormhole."

I sighed. "Got it. I best keep going then. I'll reach out after I get the second device installed."

"Please do. Be safe, Andrew."

4

Despite my obvious time crunch, I couldn't resist checking in on Hanna. It felt like it'd been ages since the two of us had spent that late evening in the library, when in fact it was only yesterday. So much had happened between then and now. I knew I should keep my focus on the triangulation devices, but I needed to see her. If for some reason this plan didn't work, I'd never see her again.

From the Orlop Deck I made my way up three flights of stairs to arrive back on E Deck. A moment later I approached cabin E-17, again greeted by Smethells. He nodded towards me.

"Good to see you again, sir," he said. "Your lady is just as she was when you left. She seems more tired, though."

Her body is wearing out from trying to fight the disease, I thought. "Has anyone else been by?"

He shook his head. "Not a soul. I believe the officers have their hands full with this darn outbreak. It's quite a mess, I must say. Thankful to be down here, away from the panicked first class."

I smiled and motioned toward the door. "Okay for me to go in?"

"Of course, sir. Mum's the word if anyone happens to come by."

I patted him on the shoulder, thankful as ever for his hospitality, as I quietly opened the door and stepped inside. Hanna was sound asleep, her entire body save for her head was covered in what few blankets were provided down here. At that moment I decided I needed to get her back up to my cabin, whatever it took. While the thought hurt, if Hanna really was on her deathbed, I certainly didn't want it to be a bunk in an E Deck cabin.

I quietly approached the bed, sitting on the edge of it. I watched as Hanna's chest rose and fell steadily as she slept. Her hair was slightly matted to her face from her fever causing her to sweat. I leaned over and kissed her forehead, which felt hot to the touch. *She's burning up.* She started awake, her surprise quickly changing to relief as our eyes met.

"Oh, Andrew," she said, putting up her arms to hug me.

She winced, the pain throughout her body evident on her face. "Sorry, I'm just so tired and weak."

I quickly embraced her. "No need to be sorry. I just needed to check in on you." I took another look at the tiny and thin bed, shaking my head. "And I'm going to get you back to my cabin. You should be as comfortable as you can be."

She pulled away and shook her head. "Andrew, no. You need to focus on saving the ship. How comfortable I am won't mean a thing if she sinks."

I was about to argue, but I couldn't deny that she had a point. If Titanic followed the course she was on, no amount of comfort would make a damn bit of difference.

I sighed and conceded. "You're right, of course." I took her hand in mine. "Do you need anything?"

She shook her head, a subtle smile forming on her face. "Go do what you need to… save this ship and all her passengers. You have an opportunity to make a huge difference in their lives… and ours."

I leaned in and carefully kissed her on the lips, avoiding the painful rashes on her face. "I love you, Hanna. I promise I'll be back as soon as it's done."

A small tear streamed down the side of her face. "I love you too. Get back to it, mister." She managed a laugh, which made me smile.

"Yes, ma'am." I winked at her and turned to leave the cabin. But, as I reached for the doorknob, I heard a familiar voice talking to Smethells in the hall.

It was Mr. King, the Master-at-Arms.

5

I felt all of the blood leave my face. My heart jumped into my throat as I turned back to Hanna. The fear must have been evident because I saw the same look appear on her face.

"What is it?" she mouthed.

"It's the Master at Arms," I whispered. "I'm hoping Smethells can talk him down." I quietly leaned my ear towards the door, desperate to hear the conversation.

"So, you haven't seen Mr. Lawson?" asked Mr. King. "I just got back from his cabin, and he was nowhere to be seen. Everyone I've spoken to has said the same thing… they haven't seen him."

Smethells responded without hesitation. "Well, it is a rather large ship, sir." This made me smirk. Although, at the same time, I realized how big of a risk I was taking by being in the cabin with Hanna. The only thing separating me from ruining everything was a single door. If King got past Smethells, I'd have nowhere to hide.

The Master at Arms scoffed. "I don't like this at all. Something strange is going on with those two. It's bad enough we have a damn outbreak among the passengers… and now one of my prisoners is running amok." I could hear the frustration in his voice.

"I don't disagree, sir," said Smethells. "Unfortunately, I haven't seen him. In fact, you're the first soul I've seen nearly all day. Dead quiet down in these parts."

I heard King grunt. "That doesn't surprise me, given the circumstances. And it's starting to get late." He sighed. "How's Mr. Lawson's lady doing?" My heart rate skyrocketed. *Don't come in, don't come in.*

"She's quite tired," said Smethells. "I checked on her moments ago, and she was in a restless sleep. Her fever is back."

Another sigh from King. "I'll have the doctor check in after I check around once more before retiring for the night. Keep a lookout for another hour or so, then you're welcome to do the same."

"Very good, sir. Let me know if I can be of more assistance."

"Good night, Smethells."

"Good night, sir."

I put my hand to my chest as I heard Mr. King's retreating footsteps. *Thank you, Smethells.* I walked back over to Hanna and kissed her goodbye again. I waited thirty seconds to ensure the coast was clear and then made my way out of the cabin.

"I owe you my life, Smethells. Thank you so much."

He shrugged. "Just doing what feels right, sir. I don't like Mr. King much, and I think he's got it out for you, for some odd reason."

I nodded. "Yeah," I began, "it's complicated."

He put out his hand in a *stop* motion. "Enough said, Mr. Lawson. The less I know the better. You best be on your way… you look like a man on a mission."

I glanced at my watch—10:40. "A mission I'm running quite late for, yes. "I put my hand out. "Thank you again, Smethells."

He shook my hand with a smile. "Of course, sir. Do take care of yourself."

With that, I made my way back up once again from E Deck, and headed for the First Class Smoking Room on A Deck to install the second triangulation device.

One precious hour remained until Titanic's date with the iceberg.

6

Even though I was in a hurry, I moved slowly and methodically throughout the ship to avoid being seen by any officers. To my relief, thanks to it being nearly eleven p.m., most of the ship was quiet. I imagined the only officers on duty would be on the bridge—which I would have to navigate around them sooner or later as well.

A few moments later I found myself in front of the smoking room's door. I felt around in my pocket to make sure I still had the devices—I did. I sighed and opened the door, the stuffy smell of smoke being the first thing to greet me. I kept myself on high alert as I walked in, taking in my surroundings. Thankfully, it was a very light crowd that evening.

At one of the larger tables were a group of men, dressed to the nines, who had been heavily drinking and playing cards. None of them paid me any attention, which was just the way I liked it. As I made my way farther into the room, I saw a familiar face—Mr. Andrews. He was seated alone, along the aft wall near one of the fireplaces.

I carried on, making a note to say hi to him before I left, and successfully installed the second device.

Mr. Andrews must have been lost in thought, because it wasn't until I sat down in the chair across from him that he recognized my presence. I could tell he wasn't himself from the get go. And I was pretty sure I knew why.

"Oh, Mr. Lawson," he said, raising his drink to me. "My apologies, I must not have seen you come in. It's good to see you again."

"You too, Mr. Andrews. I wanted to thank you for what you did... for everything you've done for me while I've been onboard." I found myself looking over my shoulder multiple times, paranoid that I'd be spotted.

He clearly noticed. "You can relax, Mr. Lawson. I promise none of the officers will be in tonight. Between the smaller night shift, and the outbreak, this is as busy as it'll get. And you're most welcome, by the way. So, how's this mission of yours going?"

I really did try to relax, but not entirely. "That's actually why I'm here. My friend, the one who sent me here, has a plan to save the ship. And he thinks it'll work."

Mr. Andrews leaned in. "Do tell."

And so, I did. I knew I didn't have much time, so I spoke quicker than I normally would have, only slowing down when he had questions—which, surprisingly, wasn't often. About fifteen minutes later, I finished and sat back in my chair, exhaling and trying to relax further.

He remained silent for a few moments before responding. "That's quite a story, Mr. Lawson. If what you say is possible, I have to ask. Will any of us notice when… 'it' happens?"

I nodded. "You will, but it'll be very brief… and it won't be painful, just a bit uncomfortable. And if passengers are asleep, I'd wager the feeling won't be long enough to wake them."

Mr. Andrews leaned back in his chair as well, thinking over everything I just dropped on him.

"There must be something else," he said. "I understand why you came here, of course, to plant one of these… uh, what'd you call them, a triangulation device?" I nodded. "But, if that was your only reason, you clearly could have done so and left without me ever seeing you."

The man didn't miss much, that was for sure. Even when

he's been told his brand new ship was going to sink on her maiden voyage, his mind was as sharp as ever.

I cleared my throat. "I might need your help one last time, if you're willing of course."

A grin formed on his face. "Come now, Mr. Lawson. You're a smart man, I know this to be true, but asking the chief designer of Titanic if he'll help save her from disaster?" He shook his head in a disappointed manner, but I could tell he was giving me a hard time by the grin that remained. "You have my word I'll do all I can. Let's hear it."

7

Ten minutes later, I shook Mr. Andrews's hand and left the smoking room. Once in the hall I checked the time—11:15. On multiple occasions it occurred to me that I had vastly wasted my precious time onboard. Four days ago I boarded Titanic, knowing all too well her fate, yet here I was, less than forty minutes to go until that very moment, and I was still working on saving her. *Love will make a man do strange things,* or something like that, I thought.

I took a seat in one of the chairs in the hallway and initiated the connection back to James. After confirming my identity, I heard a moment of static and then the sound of typing came into my ear. *That man was the loudest typer I'd ever heard.*

"James? I just got the second device installed. Can you confirm?"

"Second device confirmed. It looks good, Andrew. What took so long? You're quickly running out of time."

Don't I know it, I thought.

"Well aware of that, James. Things aren't convenient over

here. With me being a wanted man, as well as a smallpox outbreak, I have to be careful when I'm moving about."

"That'd do it," said James. "Okay, well I'll let you go. Get yourself up to the bow and install that last device. I'm concerned about having adequate time to calibrate them."

"Wait, what? I thought you said it would take five minutes."

"I said five minutes, give or take. There's a lot of calculations that need to occur here, Andrew. And if any one of them is off by the most infinitesimal of amounts, this won't work."

I sighed. "Understood. I'm off to the Boat Deck. Will be in touch again shortly."

8

I was about to head up the grand staircase to the Boat Deck, but at the last minute I decided to use the second class stairs—less obvious of a choice was my thought. As I climbed up the flight, my mind wandered from the task at hand and onto Hanna. It was crazy to think how much she meant to me after only four days of knowing her. I felt like I'd known her for years. And the best part? I could tell without question that she felt the same about me. I managed a smile as the thought of us in the future, living happily together.

I just reached the top step of the staircase when I felt a firm hand grip onto my shoulder. I immediately tensed every fiber of my body as my thoughts flew back to the present. *Hanna.* That was the only thought I had at that moment. I worried if the hand belonged to who I was almost certain it did, I'd never see her again.

"Well, look who it is," said the man. "Hello, Mr. Lawson."

I was right, of course. "Mr. King," I managed to say. I felt my heart at the base of my throat. "Listen, you have to believe me, I'm not trying to sabotage the ship… I'm trying to save her."

I was still frozen in place, standing on the top step, looking at the door leading to the Boat Deck. I felt I could actually hear Mr. King thinking how ridiculous what I just said sounded. His next response left no doubt of this.

"You really must take all of us for fools, Mr. Lawson." The silence in between talking was dreadful. "Turn around and face me."

The continued feeling of dread washed over me as I slowly turned around. And then I was face to face with the Master at Arms. He had a pair of handcuffs in his hand, but more concerning than that was the pistol I now saw that was holstered on his hip. *Will he shoot me?* I knew the answer, but didn't want to think about it. I thought about running—I almost certainly could outrun him, but not so much a bullet.

"We're running out of time, Mr. King," I said, trying to plead with him. "In less than…" I paused, wondering if it was safe to take out my watch. I chose against it. "Do you have the time?"

He let out a heavy sigh and looked at his watch. "It's 11:30, if you must know."

Shit! Where does the time go? I've never seen it move so quickly. This is going to be tight.

"Okay, this is serious, Mr. King." I think even at that moment, he might have seen something in my face, because for only a second, I saw sincere concern on his face. "Titanic is going to hit the iceberg in ten minutes. You have to believe me!" A moment later, however, the concern was long gone.

He laughed. The man actually laughed. "Sure, right. And I suppose next you'll tell me she's going to sink. Give me a break, Mr. Lawson. The Titanic is the greatest and safest ship in the world. A little berg isn't going to do her no harm."

Ugh, I thought. Of course that would be what he'd say. I knew all too well, even before going back to 1912, that those working for White Star thought the Titanic was this unsinkable giant, impervious to anything the vast oceans could throw at her. But seeing this blind naivety first-hand was something else.

"You don't understand," I said, practically begging at this point. "She's going to swipe the berg on her starboard side, and it'll punch holes into five of the watertight compartments. She will sink."

He shook his head. "Yeah, yeah. Okay, that's enough, Mr. Lawson. Turn around with your hands behind your back. You're going back down to—"

Without thinking too much about it, I shoved him backward and ran as fast as I could out the door to the Boat Deck. I heard him shout something as he tumbled down the set of stairs we'd been standing on. Did I feel bad about it? Yes, but only a little. I had much bigger things to worry about.

9

I sprinted across the deck, making my way towards the bow. I pulled out my watch and saw I only had eight minutes. *I'm not going to make it.* I shook the thought from my head and ran faster than I'd run since my high school track career. I felt my heart pounding fiercely in my chest, begging me to stop.

As I made my way farther towards the bow, I realized in my rush I'd forgotten that getting to the bow from the Boat Deck required me to go through the Officer's Promenade. *Oh well,* I thought. A moment later I scaled the gate that separated the two parts of the deck and flew down the Crew's staircase onto the A Deck Promenade. Out of the corner of my eye I thought I spotted First Officer Murdoch with a cup of tea, but I was in too big a hurry to know for sure.

I practically threw myself down the stairs leading to the Forecastle Deck. *Nearly there.* A moment later I reached the bow. I pulled the final device from my pocket and attached it to the bottom of the railing. I initiated the connection back to James, validated my identity, and waited. A moment later, I heard the typing again.

"James? James, we're out of time. I have the third device installed."

"Confirmed," he said. "Initiating calibration. Standby."

A loud *boom* rang out, rippling across the dead calm water, and was followed by an immense burning coming from my left shoulder. *Oh god, this is it. He shot me. This is how I die.*

"Don't move!" shouted a voice from behind me. "Turn around, Mr. Lawson. Turn around or I'll shoot you again."

I slowly turned, the pain in my shoulder growing with each passing second, and saw Mr. King. He had a large bruise forming on his forehead from his fall, and he was aiming his pistol at my face. *I'm so close,* I thought. *So close to ending this.*

"Listen, Mr. King, if you just give me—"

"Stop talking, Mr. Lawson. I'm so tired of listening to your crazy ramblings about the future and all that nonsense. You're in a great mess of trouble, and I think you'd be better off worrying about getting yourself legal representation."

"Andrew?" James was back in my ear. "What's going on? Was that a gunshot? Are you okay? Calibration is almost done. I need another couple minutes."

And then I heard it—the sound I'd been dreading to hear.

Frederick Fleet had just spotted the iceberg, and now the lookout bell rang three times.

"James, we're out of time," I said, ignoring Mr. King and his pistol for the moment. "Fleet just rang the lookout bell. We have less than a minute!"

Mr. King's face suddenly turned to horror. "Dear god," he said, nearly losing his grip on the pistol." He started to back away from me.

I took a chance and turned to face the bow, and then I too saw it—the infamous iceberg that sank the Titanic.

Despite what I'd seen about the iceberg in articles, interviews, documentaries, and other countless forms of media, nothing could have prepared me for seeing it in person. The mountainous block of ice quickly approached, filling up my vision as I stood motionless.

"Yo—you were telling the truth," muttered King. "How did you know?"

I ignored him, unable to pull myself from the iceberg. I felt my heart continuing to race in my chest—both from my Olympic sprint earlier and my current situation. The gunshot wound in my shoulder also wasn't helping matters in the least.

"James? What's our status? We have thirty seconds at most. And I think I'm going to pass out."

I heard the most furious typing in my ear that I'd heard so far.

"I think we'll make it," he said. "Just doing some last second calculations. I want to get this right."

Me too, I thought, but I was staring at an iceberg over three stories tall coming straight at us.

"Who are you talking to, Mr. Lawson?"

I turned quickly to Mr. King, who I saw had actually put

his pistol away. "Shut it! I'm trying to save this ship, like I've been trying to tell you the whole time."

The iceberg was unimaginably close now, and I felt the reversing engine kick in, and the ship began to turn ever so slightly towards port—but I knew it wouldn't be enough, of course.

"James? Status? We have no time."

A couple seconds of silence sent my anxiety through the roof.

And then I heard him for the last time. "Ready to go. Initiating the Anode Reactor. Coordinates are inputted. You'll be teleported to a location about seven hours outside of New York. Good luck, Andrew. Thank you for doing this. Executing in 3, 2, 1…"

The sound of static erupted in my ear. I tore the device out of my ear just before a blinding flash of light engulfed the ship. Everything, including the iceberg, vanished as my vision became flooded with the white light—and then everything went silent.

10

The sight and sound of the ocean came back as quickly as it had left. It was still the bitter cold night of April 14th, but as I looked out over the bow, I saw we were completely clear of the ice field. A smile formed on my face as I realized the plan worked. If James's coordinates were correct, and I'd bet money they were, it was about seven hours until we reached New York. We'd be arriving significantly earlier than planned, which I'm sure Mr. Ismay would be thrilled about, but more importantly the Titanic would complete her maiden voyage.

I heard several sets of footsteps approaching from behind.

I turned to see Captain Smith, First Officer Murdoch, Mr. Andrews, and Thomas King. All of them had a rather stunned expression on their faces. *This could go one of two ways,* I thought.

"Well, Mr. Lawson," said Smith. "It seems we owe you an apology." He motioned toward Mr. Andrews. "Thomas relayed to me things that you couldn't possibly know unless you really were from the future. Combined with the very real iceberg my crew reported seeing, as well as the ship suddenly being in an entirely different part of the ocean, I'd say you have indeed saved Titanic. And for that, I thank you."

He stepped forward and put out his hand. It was then he noticed my shoulder, which was still bleeding and causing me an excruciating amount of pain.

"Oh dear," he said. "You're hurt." He turned to Officer Murdoch. "Fetch the doctor immediately. I want this man treated without delay.

"Aye, sir." Murdoch made haste back towards the bridge.

I forced a smile at the captain. "You're most welcome for saving her, sir. I hope she has a long and successful career."

He smiled back and nodded. "As do I, Mr. Lawson. As do I."

11

As I had requested, Mr. Andrews had ensured that Hanna was brought back up to my cabin on C Deck. After a bit more conversation with the group on the Forecastle Deck, I went to my cabin and told Hanna the good news. She was relieved, of course, but I could tell she was suffering greatly.

"Just a few hours to go until New York," I said. "Once there we can get you the best medicine there is to offer."

She smiled at me as I held her in my arms. "But how? I was a stowaway, remember? I don't have a cent to my name."

I returned her smile in earnest. "Let me worry about that. James made sure we'd never have to worry about money ever again."

Her eyes lit up. "You mean it?"

I nodded. "Just rest now, my dear. There's something I need to attend to. I'll be back in a bit." I kissed her on the lips before leaving the cabin.

12

As I entered the First Class Smoking Room, Mr. Andrews was sitting where the two of us first talked after Titanic left Southampton. I smiled as I walked over and sat down in the chair across from him.

He held up his drink to me. "You did it, Mr. Lawson. You saved Titanic."

I smiled again. "I couldn't have done it without you."

"Nonsense," he said. "I did very little, in the grand scheme of it all."

I shook my head. "You were paramount in this plan's success, and for that I'm most grateful, sir. Thank you so much for all you did."

"You're welcome, Andrew. And thank you again for saving my ship. And for saving the lives of over 1,500 who would have been lost. Them and their families will never know the tragedy you helped prevent, but myself and all of the White Star crew will... and we won't forget it."

The two of us chatted for another hour, just about this and that, nothing of much importance. I had a few drinks with him. We laughed and had a great time. It was nearly three in the morning when I emptied my last drink.

"I should get some sleep," I said. "It's been a long day and night."

He nodded. "You must be exhausted. Go get some rest with your lady. Thanks to you, we'll be in New York very soon."

I put out my hand. "Thanks again, Mr. Andrews. It was a pleasure getting to know you."

He shook my hand. "The pleasure was all mine, Mr. Lawson. If I don't see you again before we arrive, take care of yourself and your lady. Give her my best."

I nodded, bid him farewell, and left for my cabin, C-73, onboard Titanic, the ship that did not, in fact, sink after hitting an iceberg in the North Atlantic.

EPILOGUE

STATEN ISLAND, NY, APRIL 14TH, 1918

It's been six years since I (with the help of several others) prevented the greatest maritime disaster from happening. Not a day goes by that I don't think back on my time aboard Titanic during her maiden voyage. I mean, who else can say they got the opportunity to do such a thing?

Since arriving in New York, with the immense generosity of James, I was able to get Hanna the best medical care available in 1912. It took a few months, but she fully recovered from her battle with Smallpox. The two of us now live happily in a modest home in Staten Island. She's working in a local bakery, while I stuck to my teaching roots and am teaching History to high schoolers. I'd be lying if I said I wasn't disappointed that I'd never again be able to teach students about the Titanic, but it makes me happy to know how many lives were saved by my actions that night.

As I sit in my study writing the last bit of this book, I want to make sure to include a section about James. Dr James Kern is the one who really saved Titanic. I did the footwork, of course, and if he was here I know he'd deny it, but it was his genius work on time travel and teleportation that did the heavy lifting (definitely a pun in there). I haven't heard anything from him since that night, and I doubt I ever will. But, I think about him every day and about what he did for us. I'll never forget it, James.

So, there you have it. That's the story of how a small town History teacher was thrown back in time to 1912 and saved the Titanic from sinking. It's still surreal, six years later, when I think about it. As I write this last paragraph, I'm checking my watch for the time. It's another departure day for Titanic, heading back to Southampton. Hanna and I have first class tickets. For saving her, White Star Line gave the two of us lifetime tickets, to be used at our leisure. And with that, I best get going. Thank you for coming along with me on the single greatest adventure of my life.

Titanic awaits!

ABOUT THE AUTHOR

Ben Armstrong is an emerging author of science fiction, psychologic thrillers, and general fiction. He has a love of tea, coffee, and anything related to tech. He currently resides in Washington, with his loving wife, Catrina.

Made in the USA
Monee, IL
24 May 2024

58598177R00132